M   Tapply, William G.

Dead winter

93,080

$16.95

DATE			

DEAD WINTER

WILLIAM G. TAPPLY

Delacorte Press

Published by
Delacorte Press
Bantam Doubleday Dell Publishing Group, Inc.
666 Fifth Avenue
New York, New York 10103

Library of Congress Cataloging in Publication Data
Tapply, William G.
  Dead winter: a Brady Coyne novel / William G. Tapply.
    p. cm.
  ISBN 0-385-29711-4
  I. Title
PS3570.A568D39 1989
813'.54—dc 19   88-13867
                                                     CIP

Designed by Christine Swirnoff

Manufactured in the United States of America
Published simultaneously in Canada

May 1989
10 9 8 7 6 5 4 3 2 1
BG

DEDICATION

For my dearest ones—
Sarah, Melissa, and Michael

ACKNOWLEDGMENTS

I am indebted to Rick Boyer, Cindy Tapply, and Jackie Farber for their sharp and objective ears and eyes. I am also grateful to Jed Mattes, Betsy Rapoport, Kate Mattes, and fellow members of the Cadavers for their unswerving friendship and support.

PROLOGUE

THE JANGLE of the phone dragged me up from a dead dreamless sleep. I felt the predictable panic. The question was simple: was it Billy's MG or Joey's Jeep they had found wrapped around a tree?

I groped for the phone beside my bed and got the receiver off the hook without opening my eyes.

"Coyne," I mumbled.

"Brady, it's Desmond Winter."

"Jesus, Des. What time is it?"

"I don't know. Two something. Brady, listen. I'm . . ." His voice trailed away.

I bunched my pillow under my head. "Des? Are you there?"

There was a pause. "I'm here. I'm sorry. It's just that—"

"Is it Connie? Have you heard from Connie?"

"I wish it was that." I heard him sigh. I hitched myself into a semisitting position in my bed and switched ears with the telephone.

"Come on, Des. What's up?"

"It's Maggie."

"Maggie? What about her?"

"Oh, dear. Brady, this is awful." He sighed again. I waited. He cleared his throat. "She's—she's dead, you see."

Phone calls in the middle of the night. They never bear good news. "What happened?" I said gently.

"She's been murdered, Brady. Marc called me. I figured I should call you. I'm sorry about the hour."

"Marc—?"

"They're holding him at the police station."

"Marc killed her?"

"I—no. I don't think so."

"Has he been arrested?"

I heard my old friend sigh. "I don't know. It wouldn't be the first time. As well you know. I really don't know what's going on. Marc called me. Said Maggie was dead. Murdered, that is. He said he didn't do it."

"They all do," I said before I could stop myself. "Look, I didn't mean—"

Des, to his credit, managed a short nasal laugh. "That's okay."

"I'm sure Marc . . ." I let the thought dissipate. I wasn't sure about Marc at all. I tried again. "Keep the faith, Des," I said lamely.

"Theology," he said dolefully, "seems to fail me when I need it the most."

Desmond Winter was the only retired Unitarian minister in my stable of wealthy old clients. Maggie was his daughter-in-law, the wife of his son, Marc. The couple lived with Des in his big square Federal-period house on High Street in Newburyport. They had run off to get married the previous summer after a short courtship. I met her once and remembered her as an elfin, vague woman, what the kids would call a spaceshot. But very, very attractive.

I sat all the way up, switched on the light over my

bed, and swiveled my legs around so that I could reach my shirt where I had dropped it before hitting the sack. I found the nearly empty cigarette pack in the pocket. My pants were under the bed. I fished out my faithful Zippo, got a Winston lit up, and inhaled deeply. It tasted awful.

"Tell me what happened, Des."

"I told you. I don't know." He coughed—an effort, it seemed, to regain control. "I was sleeping and the phone rang. Marc said he was at the police station. He said he found Maggie murdered and called the police and now he's there."

"Where?"

"Huh?"

"Where did he find her?"

"In the boat. He found her—her body—in the boat."

"When?"

"I don't know. Tonight sometime."

I stubbed out the cigarette half-smoked. "You want me there?"

"Can you? Will you? Will you come, Brady?" he said.

I smothered a yawn. "Of course," I said. "It'll take about an hour. Where will you be?"

"Here, I guess. At the house."

"I'm on my way. Sit tight."

Newburyport is tucked inside the good natural harbor formed by the mouth of the Merrimack River on the Massachusetts North Shore close to the New Hampshire border, where it's been for about three hundred years. It's a straight shot north from the parking garage under my bachelor's apartment on the Boston waterfront. At two on a July Monday morning, aside from a few random drunks and big ten-wheelers and weekend stragglers dragging trailered powerboats home from Maine lakes, I had the highway to myself.

I smoked Winstons as I drove and sucked on the can of Pepsi I had snagged from my refrigerator on the way out the door. It wasn't coffee, but I hoped the caffeine would get the gears churning. I passed the motels, night spots, auto dealers, and Chinese restaurants that lined Route 1, all still brightly illuminated even at that hour. When I merged onto Interstate 95 and left the city lights behind, I was able to see the heat lightning that played across the eastern horizon as I drove. A thunderstorm would have been a relief.

I shoved a Beach Boys tape into the deck, turned up the volume, and sang along with their Greatest Hits. It reminded me of those days in my youth when I would have fun, fun, fun until my daddy took my T-bird away.

Of course, in my family it had been a Chevy sedan. But Boston wasn't California, either, and anyway, the Beach Boys could sing better than I, although I did sound pretty good to myself inside my car in the middle of a steamy July night on my way to a murder.

1

D E S M O N D W I N T E R had first called me on a
rainy November day back in 1977. I was slouched at my
desk in my office in Copley Square feeling sorry for myself. It wasn't just the hard rain that ticked against the
window behind me, threatening to turn to snow, or the
premature gray dusk of the late afternoon. Nor was it
entirely the prospect of a long winter with no trout fishing or golf or any of the other worthwhile things in life.
And I couldn't truthfully blame Gloria for the mood I
was in that day, even though we had begun to discuss the
divorce that would within a couple years become a fact,
and I was finding my home no more hospitable than my
office.

It was all those things coming together at once, as
they sometimes seem to.

What I needed was a man with troubles worse than
mine to cheer me up.

"Florence Gresham suggested I call you," Desmond
Winter told me on the phone.

"Yes?"

"She said you were reliable and discreet."

"I am. Yes."

"She said you worked alone. She said that if you became my attorney, I could depend on your personal attention to my affairs."

"That's how I work."

"So I checked around."

"You sound like a discreet person yourself, Mr. Winter."

"I am. I am very careful. I have to be. I am a minister. And I am not without assets. Not that we ministers make a great deal of money, understand. My father was a banker. Very successful. I am his only heir." He cleared his throat. It conveyed an apology. "I have kept a Boston firm on retainer for many years. I have not been happy with the attention they have given me. You never know which one of those interchangeable gray people you're going to deal with. All this specialization. An expert for everything. Makes one feel as if nobody is paying any attention to the whole picture. You want something, they have to have a meeting of the partners. That style does not suit me. Anyway, I have informed them that I no longer need their services."

"And you want mine."

"Yes. Perhaps."

"Is there something specific?"

"As a matter of fact, there is. I wouldn't care to discuss it on the telephone. Can we meet?"

"We can meet," I said, "as long as you understand that I haven't agreed to take you on."

"I understand perfectly."

So I agreed to let Desmond Winter buy me lunch the following Tuesday at Locke Ober's—his choice—so we could size each other up. He turned out to be a lanky, doleful man with a shock of white hair that spilled carelessly over his forehead. He was, I guessed, close to sixty back then, a good twenty-five years older than I. He had a long neck and a protruding Adam's apple which bobbed nervously when he talked.

He drained one quick martini and made a good start on a second before I finished the single bourbon old-fashioned I usually rationed to myself at lunchtime. We shared Florence Gresham anecdotes by way of warming up for what he really wanted to discuss. When the waiter sidled deferentially up to our table, Winter waved him away. Then he leaned forward on his forearms.

"Mr. Coyne," he began, "this is a very delicate matter."

He hesitated. I nodded.

"You see, Constance, my wife, disappeared a little over six years ago."

"Disappeared?"

He shrugged. "I don't know what other word to use. She was—she is, I mean—my true love. One day—it was back in '71—I came home from the church at lunchtime, as I always did. Connie and I usually had lunch together. It was a kind of ritual for us, a quiet time when Marc and Kat—they're our children—were in school. Connie would have sandwiches or maybe chowder all prepared. We might have a touch of sherry. I'd talk about my work. She'd update me on all of her volunteer activities. She was a great volunteerer, Mr. Coyne, not just in the church—she worked with the children's choir and the altar guild—but also for many of the commissions that were working to preserve the historical landmarks in Newburyport, and the environmental groups, and school things for the kids. She's a quiet person. Ladylike. But with a lot of backbone. You'd like her." He hesitated and appealed to me with his eyes. "Everybody liked her."

I cleared my throat and nodded, noting his use of the past tense in his last statement.

Winter smiled. "I could go on and on about Connie. I

guess I tend to. You see, on this one day—it was May, a beautiful golden day, I remember distinctly, because I was going to suggest we take our sherry out onto the patio where we could look at the garden and smell the sea air—the lilacs were just coming into bloom—on this one day, Connie wasn't there. She left me a note. When I saw it lying there in the middle of the kitchen table, I didn't think too much about it. Sometimes she'd get called away, just as I would. She always left something for me to eat and a note when she wasn't going to be there."

He paused to drain his second martini. He snaked out the olive with his forefinger and popped it into his mouth. Then he looked around and caught the attention of our waiter, who hustled to our table. "Another, please," he said, holding up his glass.

"Sir?" said the waiter to me.

"What the hell," I said. It looked like it was going to be a long lunch hour. I glanced at the man sitting across from me. He was, I suddenly remembered, a minister. "Excuse my language," I said.

He smiled and waved his hand. "Please. No offense."

When the waiter left, Winter said, "The note. I will always remember what it said. 'Dearest Dizzy,' it began. It's what Connie called me, an ironic little joke between us. I am really the least dizzy person imaginable. I suppose it's a shortcoming. Connie always teased me for being so straitlaced and practical. 'Dearest Dizzy. Kat and I are leaving for a while. I know this will confuse and upset you. You must trust me that we will be back. I cannot say any more about this now except to implore you not to worry. We will be fine. Please do not try to find us or contact us. We will not contact you, either. I apologize for the mystery. When we return I will explain all. Until then remember I love you and never lose faith in me. Your Connie.'"

Desmond Winter recited this to me with the same feeling, the same resonant baritone, and the same instinct for phrasing and pausing as I subsequently observed in his sermons. It was moving to hear. I could tell that he was moved as well.

"That was six years ago?" I said.

He nodded. "Six and a half years ago, actually. Six years last May. Six painfully sad years for me."

"Kat is your daughter?"

He nodded. "Yes."

"And they still haven't returned?"

He shook his head. "Oh, Kat came back. Six years ago almost to this day. She was gone about six months. Connie wasn't with her."

"How old was your daughter then?"

"Fourteen. She's twenty now. The apple of this old man's eye, I don't mind telling you. A junior at the University of New Hampshire, majoring in, of all things, business. Marketing. Accounting. Stuff I know little and care less about. She thinks she wants to be a banker like her grandfather. Anyhow, when she arrived that day she told me that Connie had put her on a train, gave her money for a cab, and said she'd be coming right along."

"Where had she been for those six months? What were they doing?"

He shrugged. "She didn't seem to know. She was— reticent about it. As if the memory was painful."

"Did she know why her mother didn't come home with her?"

Winter shrugged. "No. Just that she'd be coming."

"And she didn't."

"No. She didn't. She still hasn't. I haven't heard a word from her."

"Have you reported this to the police?"

He lowered his head and regarded me somberly. "She asked me not to. I have honored her request." He shrugged. "I suppose I'm a difficult man to love. I'm very set in my ways. Inflexible, some would say. Rigid, even. Not only in my routines, but in my values. I am judgmental. You may think this is a shortcoming. Nowadays, firm convictions are interpreted as a sign of intellectual shallowness. But you see, I know what's right and wrong. I mean, I *know*. I have little patience with moral relativism or those who preach it. I certainly don't preach it." He frowned at me. "It's not my ministry. We Unitarians aren't necessarily like that. It's me." He jabbed his chest with his thumb. "There are guidelines. Universal truths. They're as firm as stone. You can question them and debate them and philosophize about them. Men have been doing it since Plato. You always come back to them. They are as eternal and as lawful as gravity. I adhere to them. I expect others to do the same. I always thought Connie and I were of one mind on that. We tried to bring up our children the same way. It caused conflict, sometimes. Not between me and Connie, but with the kids. Well, with Marc, mainly, as it has turned out. The minister's son. Kat has always been good."

Our drinks arrived. Desmond Winter's third, my second. He took one third of his in his mouth, tipped his head back, and swallowed. He sighed deeply. "This is difficult for me, Mr. Coyne," he said.

"Call me Brady, please."

He nodded. "My friends call me Des. I hope we will be friends."

It was a question. I shrugged. This seemed to satisfy him.

I sat back and lit a cigarette. I peered at him through the plume of smoke I exhaled. "So you assume that your wife left you because she just didn't want to remain living with you. She got tired of you. Didn't like being a minister's wife. She wanted more excitement in her life than you gave her. Probably had a lover. She brought your daughter with her, and left your boy for you. An equitable arrangement. Then she changed her mind about that and sent the girl home. The girl tied her down, probably."

He stared at me. His mouth twitched. It was hard to tell whether he was fighting tears or a smile. "You are a candid one, aren't you," he said, neither smiling nor crying. I guessed I had underestimated him. "Florence warned me about that. 'Brady doesn't pull punches,' she said. 'He'll smack you right between the eyes when you're least expecting it.' I told her that was all right with me. I've had enough of those mealymouthed smooth-as-velvet Ivy types."

I shrugged. "I got my law degree at Yale."

"Yale Law School," he said, "doesn't count."

"She walked out on you," I persisted.

He nodded. "Something like that, I guess, yes. It happens, I understand. Even in the best regulated of families." He tried a smile. He didn't look like a man who practiced smiling. "I suppose she needed time and space. I felt stupid, not to have seen it, realized it. And I felt incompetent not to have been available enough to her that she could talk to me about it. I never had a clue, Brady. One day we are loving husband and wife. The next day she's gone. Forever, it now seems."

"In her note she said she'd be back."

He made a throwaway gesture with one hand. "So I wouldn't go looking for her, right?"

I shrugged.

He hitched himself forward in his seat and removed his wallet from his hip pocket. He opened it and slid out a photograph. He held it to me. It showed a somewhat younger Desmond Winter, his hair thicker, still black, smiling self-consciously. Standing in front of him, her head resting on his shoulder and tilted back to look up at him, was a freckle-faced woman grinning with apparent affection. She wore her hair long and loose in the manner of one who had not quite outgrown hippiedom. I imagined her playing a guitar. Joan Baez songs. Smoking pot. Flowers in her hair. Bare feet. Sleeping with all the long-haired young men. Protesting war and segregation and nuclear weapons. She appeared to be ten or fifteen years younger than Des, a slim, vivacious woman.

"I know what you're thinking," said Winter to me as I examined the photo.

He arched his eyebrows, asking for my response. I handed the photo back to him. "People aren't necessarily how they appear in photographs."

He nodded. "Exactly. If Connie was that way, she surely hid it well. I never suspected. But," he said, shaking his head, "evidently I was naive in my own case."

"Your daughter. What did she tell you?"

"Not much. Nothing, really. Kat seemed traumatized by the experience, to tell you the truth. She didn't want to talk about it. She cried easily for over a year after she got back. Wouldn't even talk to her brother. I assumed she was missing her mother. They were very close. That's why Connie took Kat with her, I guess. Anyhow, I didn't push her. It really doesn't matter where they went. What matters is that Connie chose not to come back to me. And"—he spread his hands in a gesture of helplessness—"she still hasn't."

"It must have occurred to you that something has happened to your wife."

He nodded slowly. "Sure. Of course. What can I do about that? I assume that if Connie got into trouble, got injured, or—or died or something—I would be notified." He looked at me, imploring me to agree with him.

I cooperated. "Of course. Makes sense."

"Since I haven't heard anything, I assume . . ."

"That she has chosen not to return."

He nodded. "Yes."

"I'm sorry."

"Thank you. Anyway, that's the background, Brady."

I tilted up my empty glass and looked in at the yellow dregs. "Maybe we should order some food."

"I'm sorry. Of course." He lifted his head and looked around, which brought our waiter instantly.

"Gentlemen," he said. He was swarthy and somber and spoke with a Middle Eastern accent I couldn't place.

"I'll have the scrod and Bibb lettuce salad," said Winter.

The waiter nodded his approval and looked at me. I shrugged. "Sounds good. Me too."

The waiter bobbed his head and slipped discreetly away.

"This way I can say I got scrod today," said Winter. He tried a smile to let me know he had made a joke. He seemed uncertain about how I would take it.

I gave him a grin. "Let me see if I understand," I said. "Your wife has been missing for six and a half years. Now you want to track her down."

He shook his head. "No, no. That's not it. You misunderstand. It's painfully clear to me she's decided to make it permanent. If so, I must accept and respect her decision, as much as it hurts. If she should by some miracle decide to come back to me sometime in the future, I will welcome her with open arms, no questions asked. No, it's nothing like that. Last month, Brady, I received a communication from the Boss." He hesitated. "God, that is."

"I figured that's who you meant."

"A myocardial infarction. Minor, they tell me. But I'm fifty-nine years old. A small lesson on mortality is not lost on me. Do you see?"

"You want to put your affairs in order, so to speak."

"Yes. Should the Boss decide to give me the pink slip, Marc and Kat would be left with a terrible mess. Connie, of course, is the beneficiary of all my insurance. Virtually all my assets are in our joint names. I want the kids to have what's coming to them when I die without a protracted legal hassle. And I want to get this squared away without a protracted hassle from my attorney. Protracting hassles is what Flynn and Barrows are best at. Florence Gresham said that this sort of thing was right up your alley."

"It is. It's the sort of thing I do."

He held out his hands, palms up. "Well?"

I frowned. "It's kind of interesting, actually." I looked up at him. "Easiest thing would be to get yourself a divorce."

He recoiled from this as if I had shaken a fist at him. "Never. Absolutely not." He sighed. "I guess I've made a mistake. I'm terribly sorry to have bothered you, Mr. Coyne."

I smiled at him. "Ah, take it easy, Des." I reached across the table and put my hand on his wrist. "I was testing you."

He blinked. "I don't get it."

"You have insisted that you continue to love your wife. That you'd accept her back, no questions asked. I assume that if she should return upon hearing of your death, you'd want her well taken care of."

He nodded. "I thought I told you that."

"You did. And if you were telling me the truth, you would refuse a divorce."

"Which I did." He frowned for an instant, then widened his eyes at me. "You doubted my veracity." There was a note of incredulity in his voice, as if the idea was inconceivable.

"Your sincerity, Des. I'm big on sincerity. It's not something that is necessarily required between a lawyer and his client. But it is required between this particular lawyer and his clients. Of course," I added, "it works both ways."

1

He gave me a smile, the first genuine one he had allowed himself. "Florence said you'd find a way to check me out."

"It's a weakness of mine. I insist on knowing where I stand with those who want my services. In the short run, it costs me some business. In the long run, it makes the business I do have more pleasant for me. My own pleasure is important to me."

He rolled his eyes. "And I thought *I* was straitlaced."

"I prefer to think of it as principled." I smiled and extended my hand to him. "If you still want me, I'd be happy to work with you," I said.

He grinned and grasped my hand. "I absolutely do."

2

REARRANGING Desmond Winter's estate posed no problem. It was simply a matter of asking him the right questions, figuring out what he wanted, and translating it into words that others trained in the peculiar argot of the law would all understand the same way.

To accomplish this, one simply has to find ways to say things that those not trained in the language of the law find impossible to understand. It's what makes us lawyers necessary. We're about the only ones who can figure out what any of the others are saying.

It's not hard. They teach us how in law school. *Whereby*s and *whereas*es, a few *parties-of-the-second-parts*. Judicious use of semicolons. The odd Latin phrase.

This was my work, my chosen profession.

It usually bored the hell out of me. Since my peculiar niche in the legal scheme of things failed to interest me, I tried to compensate by selecting clients who did. Clients like Des Winter.

Fortunately, my chosen profession didn't interfere too much with my pursuit of brown trout and golf scores in the seventies. In fact, my profession subsidized those pursuits. It also paid Gloria's alimony, the college tuition for Billy, my number one son, who tended to squander it, and it would take care of Joey's in a couple years, too. Joey wouldn't squander it.

Des and I inevitably became friends. That's what I was checking for that day at Locke Ober's—the possibility that I would be able to like and respect the man who wanted to become my client. I have fired clients whom I lost respect for, or who liked to cut too close to the cutting edge of legality, or whom I just didn't enjoy being with. Life is too damn short.

In many respects, Des Winter was not a likely prospect to become my friend. For one thing, he turned out to be a prude, an indictment to which he freely confessed and about which he made no apology. While, for example, he acknowledged that the famed Massachusetts blue laws were a violation of any civilized concept of privacy, he agreed with every one of them as appropriate rules of conduct. Adultery, of course, was a sin. Period. Not far behind came cohabitation. Public displays of affection offended him.

He liked to tell what he considered jokes. They typically bore on theological themes. They mostly took the form of riddles. They tended to embarrass the listener, especially since Des had a short repertoire and a poor memory of whom he had run through it with.

For example: Q—Who was the fastest runner in the Bible? A—Adam. He was first in the human race.

Or: Q—How do you make holy water? A—You boil the hell out of it.

Knee-slappers. But it was hard not to love the man, dumb jokes and all.

I went to hear him preach a few times after I began to work with him and realized that I liked him very much. I found his theology more liberal, if anything, than my own, and strangely at odds with his personal ethic. He was, he told me, a Deist, a believer in a concept he said was popularized by Benjamin Franklin, and which postulated a universe like a clock—wound up by a God who then sat back bemusedly to wait for it to wind down. He took the Unitarian postulate—which denied the divinity of the Trinity—and pushed it to the edge of atheism. He advocated good works not, as the Calvinists would have had it, as a hedge against damnation, but as the moral obligation of a civilized human being. Theology had nothing to do with it. But it was the essence of religion.

I found Des Winter's homilies provocative and disturbing right up to his last one on Easter Sunday of 1982.

"I doubt if Jesus of Nazareth appeared on that day," he said. "I do not doubt that some people wanted him to do it so desperately that they were willing to imagine it. If he did, it would be a miracle. It's dangerous to live for miracles. It makes us lazy and immoral."

Although Desmond Winter practiced what he preached as well as any man I ever knew, he never was able to suspend his belief that Connie would one day return to him, even though he freely admitted it would be a miracle.

I am proud to say that I didn't learn Des owned a thirty-eight-foot Bertram named *Constance,* which he moored at a marina in Newburyport and from which he loved to troll for striped bass and bluefish, until after I had agreed to take him on as a client. *Constance* was a gorgeous craft, with a flying bridge and outriggers and berths for six and twin Cummins diesels, and I fear I could easily have compromised the rigorous standards I held for admitting new clients to my roster had Des told me about her earlier.

Des was an agreeable companion on a fishing boat. He loved and respected the sea and the fish we chased. He taught me how to recognize the distinctive odor of a school of rampaging blues, and he was as happy as I was to switch over to a fly rod when we got into them and to release all but the one or two we might want for the table.

On those long lazy cruises in the mouth of the Merrimack and around Plum Island when the fish weren't biting, I'd go forward to where Des was navigating with beers for both of us (for as otherwise rigidly upright as Des Winter was, he liked booze and handled it with gentility). He was more relaxed out on *Constance,* and while his repertoire of jokes didn't change, he seemed to appreciate mine.

But I often caught him staring unfocused out at the horizon, and I knew what he was looking for. Connie. It was as if he expected her one day to rise from the sea, much as Jesus was said to have risen from the dead.

I'd nudge him and hand him a chilled can, and he'd shake himself and grin. "I was thinking about her," he'd say. "Wondering where she is, what she's doing. Hoping she's happy."

And I'd squint into the distance. There was nothing to say.

Sometimes he'd talk about his kids, and while he didn't complain—it was not in his nature to complain— he often mused on how they might have turned out had their mother been there to help raise them. Des regarded himself as inept at parenting, and blamed himself—never the wayward Connie—for his offspring's shortcomings.

Kat, who he said had been a happy laughing child, overnight became a solemn, brooding young woman, given to long angry silences that seemed unprovoked and arbitrary to the people around her. She studied hard, almost defiantly, as if she had to prove herself worthy of the love of a mother who had abandoned her. She was a college student when I first met her. She regarded me suspiciously and resisted my mild efforts to crack her defenses. At first I found her disturbingly introverted, a young woman with a grudge against the world. It took a long time for us to become friends.

When she graduated, she got a job with a small advertising firm in Newburyport. She found a condominium near the waterfront and moved out of Des's big old house. Within three years she had her name on the company letterhead.

Kat had a face that would have been considered beautiful had she chosen to smile more often—a sprinkle of freckles across the bridge of her nose, reddish blond hair cut short and efficient, a wide mouth, large green eyes. She was tall like Des and almost too thin.

She wore tailored suits to work, and blue jeans and men's shirts otherwise. I thought she looked much better in jeans.

Her business partner divorced his wife to marry Kat. It lasted less than a year. Des asked me to handle her divorce. Kat Winter then sold out her share of the business to the heartbroken young man and set up her own competing agency, and I handled the mechanics of it.

For a long time she refused to call me anything except Mr. Coyne. I called her Miz Winter.

One March afternoon when I was in Newburyport to deliver some papers to her, I casually suggested supper at the Grog, a local restaurant featuring Cajun-style blackened fish that brought tears to my eyes. Kat, in her tweed suit, peered over her reading glasses at me and gifted me with one of her rare smiles. "Why, Mr. Coyne," she said. "Are you asking me for a date?"

"No way," I replied promptly. "You are not a fun person. You are a client. And, may I add, a client whom I would not have taken on had I not been asked to by your father. I simply thought that we have a great deal to discuss if you really want to incorporate, and that I am getting hungry. Ergo, we can kill two birds with the same rock. If you eat supper with me, I can write off the whole thing, which will take the sting out of it."

She snatched her glasses from her face. Her green eyes glittered. She said, "Well, damn you . . ." And then she paused, cocked her head, and grinned. "Yes, damn you. Okay. Strictly business, of course. I mean, if you don't want to fool around."

"I don't fool around with my clients," I said primly.

"Oh, I'll bet."

"They're mostly too old."

Kat and I didn't fool around at all. But we lingered at the Grog late that night. She drank stingers and I sipped Harvey's Bristol Cream and we talked about Des, and somewhere along the way I began to call her Kat and she called me Brady.

Her condo was a half mile from the restaurant. A cold breeze was coming off the waterfront and funneling down the street at us, so that we had to angle our bodies into it to keep our balance as we walked. After we had walked a block, Kat grabbed onto my arm. A block later she shifted her arm around my waist, and she leaned against me, burying her face against the side of my shoulder. It was natural that I would throw my arm around her.

When we got to her door, she turned, standing one step higher than I. "Want to come in and thaw out? I can make coffee."

I shook my head. "Not a good idea."

She smiled. "You don't have to think of me as a client, you know. You're off the clock now."

"I am fully aware of all that."

"Yes," she said. "I'm sure you are."

She tilted her head and brought her mouth against mine. It was a dry, tentative kiss, and I pulled away from it before it could evolve into something different. "Nothing wrong with being friends," I said.

She shrugged. "However you want it."

"Otherwise . . ."

She nodded. "Sure."

After that night we usually planned our business meetings so that we could eat together afterwards. I found her intelligent and knowledgeable. She never mentioned her mother, and I never asked about her. I had the feeling that she had dug a deep hole into her soul, buried all feelings about Connie there, and piled layers of self-control over it.

Des's son, Marc, was a year older than Kat, a dark, unpredictable, handsome young man. He was twenty-one when I first began to work with Des. When Connie Winter disappeared with Kat, Marc quit high school and fled to Augusta, Maine, where he pumped gas. Soon after Kat returned to Newburyport, Marc wandered back to the big house on High Street. After Kat left for college, Des and Marc continued to live there. They were both private, unyielding men, and they got along awkwardly. They seemed to baffle each other. Marc tended bar at one of the local watering holes, repaired marine engines, and spent a lot of time aboard *Constance*. He kept the engines tuned and the brass polished and conducted much of his social life aboard her. He talked about getting his skipper's license so he could take out charters, but he never seemed to get around to it.

The summer he turned twenty-five Marc married the daughter of a history professor from Duke, who made the mistake of docking in Newburyport on a summer family jaunt. Marc took his new bride and several of their friends on an extended cruise up the coast by way of a honeymoon. On their return home when they tied up in Newburyport they were boarded by a contingent of state and local police, Coast Guard, and DEA agents, who held Marc and his crew at gunpoint while they searched *Constance*.

They found a brick of cocaine the size of a one-pound box of Fanny Farmer chocolates wrapped in watertight plastic in the bilge. It was the first place the agents looked.

Des called me, and I got Xerxes Garrett to handle Marc's case. The others got their own lawyers and went to trial together. All of them, including his bride, claimed ignorance and pointed their collective finger at Marc. The prosecuting attorney produced a witness who was prepared to testify that Marc had approached him with an offer to set up a pipeline from Portsmouth to Fall River. Zerk plea-bargained away all but six months of relatively easy time at MCI Shirley for Marc.

When Marc went inside, his wife returned to Virginia. Her father, the professor, got the nuptial bond annulled.

After the trial and the appeal, Zerk told me, "I kinda like the dude. No bullshit about him. Told me he was set up. I told him we had no proof of that, we'd lose in court with all those witnesses fingering him. He understood right away. Told me to do what I could. Which is what I did. He thanked me afterward. Told me I was smart for a nigger. I told him he better learn how to talk to dusky-hued folks quick before he went inside, got his rectum reamed. He kinda grinned and called me sir. Good kid. Fucked up, though."

Des used to say, by way of apology for Marc, "What can you expect? He was the one Connie left behind."

I visited Marc at Shirley once. They gave us a cubicle furnished with a table bolted to the floor and wooden chairs. A guard stood inside the door watching us.

"You look good," I told him.

"Doing some lifting. Not a hell of a lot else."

"Write to your father."

"Is that an order?"

"It's a suggestion."

He shrugged. "Not much to say."

"Tell him you're all right, that's all."

"Maybe I will."

He gazed past me toward the guard. "I figured it out," he told me after a moment. "Took me a long time."

"Figured out what?"

"Who stashed the coke on *Constance.*"

"You're telling me you didn't."

"That's what I told Garrett, and I think he believed me. The fact that I let him plea-bargain don't mean I did it."

"Who, then?"

"The fuckin' professor. Bowen. Debbie's old man."

"What makes you think so?"

"Process of elimination. I didn't. Debbie didn't. None of the others would've. He hated me, hated me and Debbie being married. She wouldn't listen to him, so he showed her what kind of a person I was." He laughed ironically. "Thing was, I gave up all that stuff for her. Promised I'd live clean, get a real job. I loved her, see, Brady." He narrowed his eyes and shrugged in the unmistakably characteristic manner of one who has learned how to survive in prison. "There's a lesson somewhere. I ain't all that well educated. But I'm figuring it out."

"Don't make too much of it, Marc," I told him. "Professor Bowen is one man—even if you're right about him."

"I got plenty of time to work on it," he said.

When Marc got out of prison, he returned to live with Des. He couldn't get his bartending job back, so he hung around the marina doing odd jobs and complaining that no one would hire a guy who'd done time. He finally landed a job as a bouncer at one of the strip joints that are scattered along Route 1 north of Boston, the suburban equivalent of the combat zone. That's where he met Maggie.

Marc married her the summer before she died. I met her only once, that same summer. Des and I had planned to take *Constance* on a bluefish hunt around Plum Island. When I joined him at the marina where she was moored, I found Marc there, along with a slender girl wearing cutoff blue jeans and the top to a bikini.

"Ah, Brady Coyne, this is Maggie," said Marc. "My wife," he added, grinning at the young woman as if it were a private joke.

She had a great cascade of coal black hair, very large eyes the color of hot fudge, and an infectious smile. She was standing next to Marc on the dock, one arm draped possessively over his shoulder. She was nearly his height, close to six feet, and looked to be about his age. They could have been twins with their deep tans and dark flashing smiles. "Nice to meetcha," she said. "Hope you don't mind us messin' up your fishing."

I assured her that nobody messed up my fishing except perverse fish.

Marc took the wheel and steered us out into the estuary where the Merrimack met the ocean. Des and I trolled Rebels while Maggie sat next to Marc. It was a still, hot day, and Marc couldn't put us onto the blues. Des and I drank beer and stared at the sea. He had the faraway look on his face that told me he was thinking about Connie. I didn't intrude.

After a while I went forward to sit on the bulkhead to catch a breeze. A few minutes later Maggie joined me. She squatted beside me and shucked off her shorts, which briefly startled me until I saw that she had the bottom to her bikini underneath.

"So you're a lawyer, huh?" she said.

"Yes. A lawyer."

"I'm a dancer," she offered.

"Mm."

"Did a lot of ballet when I was a kid. I got too big for that, though. Went through a fat stage when I was about twelve. Gotta keep working on my weight. Lot of people, they don't think the kind of dancing I do is really, you know, dancing."

I sipped my beer and watched a ruckus of gulls circle off toward the beach.

"Okay, so I'm a stripper," she persisted. She put her hand on my arm. I turned to look at her. Her eyes were earnest. "You probably think—"

"I don't judge people, Maggie."

She smiled. "Everybody judges strippers, Mr. Coyne. I don't wanna make it more than it is, see. We take off our clothes, and the guys, they get their jollies. But there's kind of an art to it. I mean, you gotta look right, sure. But there are girls, they got great bods, and if they can't dance, the guys, they get bored. I mean, anyone can stand there and flop their boobs around, pretend to hump someone. When I do it, I don't think about what the guys are thinkin'. I think about the music, moving to it, trying to be graceful and pretty and sexy."

I shrugged.

"Look," she said. "I mean, I've got small breasts, actually, compared to most of 'em. But I've got great legs and a good ass and I know how to dance. The guys like me. They always give me a good hand. They don't say dirty things to me, like they do to some of the girls. At least, not usually. Anyhow, I quit dancing. I just did it for the money. Now Marc's takin' care of me. How old are you, anyhow?"

I told her. She cocked her head at me. "Jeez, I would've said two, three years older'n that."

"Most people think I look younger than I am," I said, feigning hurt feelings.

"Aw, jeez, I'm sorry. Things like that, they just come

out of my mouth. I'm kinda stupid that way. It must be exciting, being a lawyer. You rich?"

"Moderately rich. Not very exciting. Lots of paper-work."

"I hate paperwork. Did lousy at school."

And she went on that way, her mind skipping discon-nectedly from thought to thought, things coming out of her mouth in a random fashion that I found both discon-certing and charming.

Before the day ended, I decided that I liked her. And later Des confided in me, with some perplexity, that he liked her, too. "You'd never know she had been a, ah, performer, Brady. Quiet, well-mannered, considerate of her old father-in-law, and a dutiful wife. Reminds me a bit of Connie, actually. That same ingenuous, unpreten-tious quality. A little girl, really. That stage that com-pletely passed over Kat."

Now Maggie had been killed, and Marc was being held, and I wondered if it was possible that Marc was not guilty.

I recalled one other thing Des had said that day on the boat with Marc and Maggie when the bluefish didn't bite. "I wish," Des said of Marc's new bride, "that my son treated her better."

So I tooled through the summer night, remembering the dead stripper and singing about Good Vibrations with my Beach Boys tape.

The vibrations I was feeling were decidedly not good.

3

ORANGE LIGHTS glowed from the first-floor windows of Des's house. Kat's new Saab 9000 Turbo was parked behind a battered Dodge pickup that I assumed belonged to Marc. In front of the truck was Des's new Buick Skylark. I pulled in behind the Saab. It was sleek and fast looking. My little BMW looked positively dowdy next to it.

I went around to the back door. I tapped on the glass with my knuckles, then went inside. Des's old basset hound, Barney, was lying on a tattered rug beside the kitchen stove. He thumped his tail a couple times when he saw me and then propped himself up on his stubby legs. He bellied over to me. He moved like a snake. His body moved first and then his skin seemed to follow along. He reminded me of a Slinky. I reached down and tickled his ears. He rolled his rheumy eyes at me.

"Anybody home?" I called.

"In here," came Des's voice.

I went into one of the sitting rooms, of which there were three. Des and Kat and Marc were all there, sitting at opposite corners of the room, sipping from mugs and studying the patterns on the big oval braided rug. It didn't appear that they had been talking. Barney pushed past me. He went over to Des and flopped down beside his chair. Des reached down and absentmindedly stroked his belly. Then he looked up at me.

"Thanks for coming, Brady."

I held my hand to him and he took it. His hand felt thin in my grip.

"You call, I come."

He nodded. He was wearing a brown cardigan with frayed cuffs over an undershirt. He had on wrinkled chino pants and bedroom slippers. He looked old. "After I called you I called Kat. She went and got Marc."

I went over to Kat, who was tucked into a big wing chair with her feet under her. She lifted her face and smiled at me. "You have come to save us," she said.

I leaned down and kissed the corner of her mouth. She touched my face. "You're looking smashing, Kat," I said. No lie. She was wearing white jeans, which stretched taut against her hip and thigh. Her lime green velour pullover picked the color from her eyes.

I looked at Marc. "I'm very sorry."

"It's terrible. It makes no sense."

"They didn't arrest you, I deduce."

He nodded. "Clever you."

I shook hands with him and then sat in a vacant rocking chair. "Tell me what happened," I said to Marc.

"Somebody killed Maggie. I found her dead in the boat. I called the cops. They came and took me to the station. They ignored me for a while. Then one of them took me into a room. I asked if I could call my father. Figured they wanted to arrest me or something. After I made the call, the cop asked me a few questions. I answered them. When I was done he said I could go. Kat was waiting for me. Took me back to pick up the truck. Came back here." He shrugged.

"That's it?"

"That's it. For now. I figure maybe tomorrow they'll get their act together. I've done time, makes me a killer, right?"

"We're having tea," said Kat. "Want some?"

I waved my hand. "Don't get up."

She shrugged. "Okay."

"Get Brady some tea, Kat," said Des. "He drove all the way up here in the middle of the night. The least we can do is give him some tea."

"I was going to," she said brightly. She unfurled herself from her chair and left the room.

"Did they treat you all right?" I said to Marc.

He nodded. "Can't say they gave me a lot of sympathy. I mean, you find your wife murdered . . ." He stared down at the carpet for a moment. "I talked to a cop named Fourier. He's one of the detectives. I talked voluntarily. He listened and made some notes. When I was done he told me my sister was waiting. She took me back to my truck, and we came here. We've been sitting here sipping Constant Comment and avoiding the subject."

"Did you kill Maggie?" I said.

"No."

Kat came back in. She handed me a mug. I took it and sipped. "It's tea," I said.

"What did you expect?"

"I figured tea was a euphemism."

"You want a drink?"

"This tastes good, actually." I turned to Marc. "Why don't you tell me what happened, and what you told the police."

Des cleared his throat and stood up. Barney flopped onto his feet and looked up at Des. "I think we should leave you two. I'm going back to bed." He looked down at Marc. "Son, I'm sorry. It's an awful thing."

Marc shook his head. "Please don't think . . ."

Des touched his shoulder. "I don't."

"Brady . . ."

"Try to get some sleep, Des."

Kat went to him and they exchanged hugs and kisses. Then Des left the room. Barney scuttled along behind him.

"That," said Kat, "was a hint for me." She was standing beside my chair. She ran her fingers absentmindedly through my hair. "Good night, Brady. Nice to see you."

"I parked behind you."

"I'm staying here for the night. Wouldn't want to miss the excitement."

"She wants to take care of our father," said Marc to me.

Kat snapped a glance at Marc. It contained meaning I couldn't read. Then she bent and kissed my forehead. "G'night."

"Night," I said.

I waited until she was out of the room. Then I turned to Marc. "You're not getting a lot of sympathy from Kat."

He shrugged. "Never have. Ever since our mother left."

I nodded. "So. What happened? And what did you tell the cops?"

"I told the police what happened. The same thing."

"Tell me what you left out, too."

"Are you grilling me?"

"They're going to talk to you some more. You're right. They know you spent half a year in Shirley. When wives get murdered, ninety percent of the time it's the husbands who do it. You discovered the body. I bet someone sometime overheard the two of you arguing. You'll be a suspect tomorrow. Actually, you're undoubtedly a suspect tonight. I want to know whether to call Zerk

Garrett. If they end up arresting you, you'll need him. Otherwise I can take care of your rights."

"Okay," he said. He shifted in his chair. He was wearing gray dress slacks, a blue and white checked sport shirt, with a blue blazer. He had on black loafers with tassels, the kind of shoes I wouldn't be caught dead in. He crossed his right ankle over his left knee and plucked at the crease in his trousers. "I couldn't get to sleep. There was some thunder rumbling off in the distance. I thought of *Constance*. I had her out yesterday. Couldn't remember snugging the bowlines. Figured I probably did, but I got it into my mind that I didn't. Know how it is? You maybe can't remember unplugging the coffee pot, and even though you know you always unplug the coffeepot, once you get it into your head that maybe you didn't, you know you won't rest easy until you go back and check. I was halfway to Springfield once and that happened to me. Had to turn around. Anyway, hearing the thunder, knowing the tide was coming in and all, I couldn't get to sleep thinking about the boat smashing against the other boats. So I lay there for a while, and the longer I lay there the more I was positive I hadn't secured her. The only way I was going to get any sleep was I had to go check on her. So I did."

"Where was Maggie while you were lying there worrying about the boat?"

He looked away from me. "Out. She was out."

"Out?"

He nodded. "Out."

"I bet the police asked you where Maggie was."

"Sure. I told Fourier she was out. That we didn't keep track of each other. She had her life, I had mine. Parts of them intersected, parts didn't. It worked well for us. We did some things together. Some things apart. Maggie had her friends. They weren't necessarily my friends. So, yeah, she was out. Said she was going to have dinner with some friends, probably be out late. That was no problem. Except one of her friends killed her, I guess."

"And you don't know who these so-called friends were?"

"No, not really. Maybe people from where she used to work."

"Where's that?"

"The Night Owl. Up there on Route 1."

"The strip joint."

He shrugged. "It's what she used to do. Strip. You know that."

"That's how you met her, right?"

"Yes."

"So you think she was out with someone from the Night Owl."

"I don't know. Maybe. That was her crowd."

"Okay. Go on with your story."

"You want a beer?"

"I'd love a beer."

Marc got up and went into the kitchen. I followed him. He opened the door of the refrigerator. "Coors or Bud?"

"Bud."

He handed a bottle to me. I twisted off the cap. We sat at the kitchen table. He had a Coors. I lit a Winston and slugged from the bottle.

"I took the truck down to the marina. You remember, it's only about five minutes from here. I went out onto the docks. They're humping up and down. Strong tide coming in. Lightning flickering out over the river. Sharp, damp breeze like there's a storm coming in. Found the bowlines secure, naturally. But I noticed the hatch was open and the little light below was on. Not like me, to leave the hatch open. If the rain came, every-thing'd get soaked down there. So I hopped aboard and went below to turn off the light, see if anything'd been stolen. And Maggie was there." ⤙

He paused, sipped from his can of Coors, and stared at me over the rim.

"Dead," I said helpfully.

"Oh, man," he said softly. "I guess she was. I didn't try to find her pulse or anything."

He stopped. I got up and rummaged through the cupboards for an ashtray. I gave it up and flicked my ash into the sink. I stood there leaning back against it holding my bottle of Budweiser in one hand and my Winston in the other. Marc drew circles in the condensation on the side of his beer can.

"How did she die?" I said.

He turned his head to look at me. "It was messy. Jesus. Her—her head. It was smashed in. A big dent in her forehead. Eyes wide open and all bulgy. Blood all over the place. God!"

I turned on the faucet and doused my cigarette. I went back to the table.

"Where was she? On the floor?"

He cleared his throat. "She was sort of sprawled half in and half out of one of the berths. She was naked. Just a blanket sort of half over her. Looked like she had been sleeping and somebody came in and she sat up so the blanket fell off her. Then they smashed her on the head."

"Then what did you do?"

"I went to the pay phone. There's one there by the shop there at the marina. I called the cops and waited until they came. Which they did in about two minutes. I took them to the boat. They wouldn't let me go aboard. They looked around. I stood on the dock with a cop whose job was to make sure I didn't jump into the river or something. Then more cruisers came. And an ambulance and a couple unmarked cop cars. Then they put me into a cruiser and took me to the police station.

Fourier came along a couple minutes later. He's a guy I've known for a long time. Typical cop. The cops in this town, they look at me funny. Out of the corners of their eyes. Just reminding me they know I did time. Anyhow, Fourier took me into an interrogation room. I reminded him I had the right to make a phone call. He told me I was being premature, that they weren't arresting me or anything, but it was perfectly okay with him if I made a call anyway. So I called my father. He said he was going to call you. I told him fine. Then I talked with Fourier."

"Did he ask you any tough questions?"

Marc cocked his head at me. "Like what?"

"Like, when you got out of bed at twelve-thirty ayem and decided to go down to the boat, why you wore a sport coat and tasseled loafers?"

He frowned, then shook his head. "No, he didn't ask me that."

"But he probably will."

He nodded. "Probably. I'll tell him the truth. I was wearing these duds during the day. They were on the chair where I left them when I went to bed. First clothes I came upon in my room."

"Thin," I said.

He shrugged.

"You were in the house all night?"

"Yes."

"Was Des home?"

"Yes. I watched TV with him for a while. He went to bed a little after nine, as usual."

"When did you go to bed?"

"Eleven, maybe. I read for a little while. Turned off the light but couldn't sleep, like I told you."

"So no one can say where you were between nine and around twelve-thirty."

He stared at me for a minute and then stood up. "You want another beer?"

"Sure."

Marc went to the refrigerator and took out another Bud for me and Coors for himself. He returned to the table, cracked the can, and tipped it up. His throat worked. Then he put the can on the table and wiped his mouth with the sleeve of his sport coat. "I have no witnesses, Brady. No alibi. When my father goes to bed, he goes to sleep. He snores. Nothing wakes him up. Maggie and I have a room at the opposite end of the hall from him. There's a stairway at each end and in the middle. There are six bedrooms up there, okay? It's like living in a separate building. He can verify I was home when he went to bed. That's it. I could've sneaked out after I heard him sawing wood up there, went to the boat, found Maggie in it, and whacked her. But I didn't."

"So who did?"

He flapped his hands. "I have no idea."

"Who didn't like her?"

"I don't know anybody who didn't like her."

"Somebody from the—what was it called?"

"The Night Owl?"

"Right. The Night Owl. Anybody from there?"

"I don't know. She never mentioned enemies."

"Old lovers?"

"She probably had lots. I don't know who they were."

"What about her family?"

He shook his head. "I don't know."

"You don't seem to know much about your wife, Marc."

He smiled at me. "No, I guess not. But what I did know, I liked a lot."

"Be that as it may—"

"Look, okay? I saw her dance. She moved nice. Not like a lot of them, they just stand there and play with their tits and pretend they're humping somebody. Maggie really danced. After she was done, got dressed, she came out, sat at the bar. Couple guys put a move on her. Two bikers, looked like. Long greasy hair, grubby beards, black T-shirts with the sleeves hacked off to show their biceps and tattoos. I was watching. Just casually. I mean, first I was watching this chick move around naked, all these guys yelling to her and her joking back at them, cool, in control, smiling, taking their dollar bills when they held them to her, giving them a quick peek at her snatch. Then she comes out in slacks and blouse, looks like an ordinary person. Clean and pretty. Anyway, I'm watching her at the bar because she's more interesting than the next naked one on the stage, and the two bikers sit down on either side of her. I can't hear what they're talking about. But suddenly one of the guys jumps up like he's been shot. Then the other one kind of straightens up and backs off his barstool. The two bikers leave. Walk right out the door, looking like they'd eaten a mouthful of live bugs. So I went over and sat beside her. She was sipping some kind of fancy drink. Pink, with froth on top of it. I said to her, 'How'd you do that? What'd you say to those guys?' She grins at me and shows me what she's got in her hand. It's one of those old-fashioned hatpins, about six inches long. 'I didn't say anything,' she said to me. 'I just shoved this thing into one of their stomachs. Only about an inch. It discouraged them.' "

Marc smiled at me. "Love at first sight," he said.

"So you married her."

He shrugged. "It was a lark, really. It wasn't as if we had long intense conversations about responsibility and commitment and death doing us part. Child-rearing philosophies. Life insurance. Nothing like that. Maggie and I weren't permanent. We both understood that. Nothing was permanent with Maggie. She lived for the day. Just liked to have fun and not worry about things. She told me she did a lot of drugs one time, but they didn't make her happy. Funny kid. I mean, you think this girl, takes her clothes off and lets guys look at her, you'd think she didn't care much about herself. But she did. Ate raw vegetables, bran cereal. Didn't smoke. Drank very little. Did aerobics. She was happy to move in here. Seemed thrilled that she'd be taken care of for a while, didn't have to strip. Quit at the Night Owl. She liked living here. She liked my father a lot. Seemed happy enough keeping house, being taken care of. She liked to grub around in the gardens, watch the soaps, vacuum, make lunch for the old man. He seemed to take a shine to her. She went her way, I went mine. Sometimes we went the same way."

"Not anymore," I said.

"Look," he said. "I'm really sad she's dead. And the sight of her, all distorted, her head caved in. It was awful, and I've seen bad things. When I was inside I saw a guy, his balls and his pecker had been cut off by a jealous lover or something, poor bastard was screaming, blood all over the place. I thought I'd never see anything worse. This tonight, this was worse. Because, I guess, because it was Maggie. She knew how to take care of herself, Brady. It's upsetting. But we weren't really what you'd call in love with each other. After Debbie, I don't know if I'll ever be in love."

"And you didn't kill her."

"Honest to God, I didn't."

"Cops'll think you did."

He nodded. "I expect so. My father does. So does Kat."

"You don't mind me saying so," I said, "I've got my doubts myself."

4

I TALKED WITH MARC until about four thirty in the morning and then went to bed in one of the many bedrooms upstairs. It took me a long time to get to sleep. A soft rapping on the door awakened me. Sun was streaming in through the windows.

"Come in," I said.

The door pushed open and Kat stuck her head in. "Are you decent?"

"People have said that of me, yes. A decent sort, that Coyne."

"Is your body covered?"

I pulled the sheet up to my chin. "Yes, but I'll give you a peek if you want."

She came into the room. She was wearing a pale yellow linen suit with a printed blouse under it, matching yellow heels. No stockings on her tanned legs. I gave her a wolf whistle.

She put a mug of coffee on the table beside my bed and ignored the whistle. "I've got to get to the office," she said. "Can I move your car?"

"Keys're in the pocket." I pointed at the tumble of clothing on the floor.

She bent to them and extricated the car keys. "I'll leave them in the ignition."

"Fine. And thanks for the java."

She came over and sat on the edge of the bed. Her bottom pressed against my hip. "I didn't use to like you, you know," she said.

"We were all younger then."

"No, I mean, I had this idea that you were out to get Daddy to do something he didn't want to do. About my mother, I mean. I didn't trust you. I guess I didn't trust anybody." She smiled. "You turned out to be a nice guy."

"I was a nice guy all the time." I reached for the mug of coffee and sipped it. It gave my life new meaning.

"Well, anyway," she said, "I appreciate what you're doing. For Daddy, I mean. We don't expect miracles here."

"You think Marc killed Maggie?"

"Look," she said, frowning. "He's my brother, okay? But he's done nothing but cause Daddy heartache. Ever since . . ."

"Ever since your mother left."

She made a throwaway gesture with her head. "You get to the point, don't you? Yes. Since then."

"While you—?"

"I," she said, "have done my best to live up to my father's expectations."

I blew across the top of my coffee and peered at her. "I expect Marc has done his best, too."

"God help us if this is his best," she said softly. She stood up. "Anyway, I'm off. See you around, maybe?"

"Maybe. Have to see what happens today."

"Lunch?"

"Probably not. If Marc doesn't need me, I'll have to get to the office."

"Sometime, then."

"Sometime."

Kat left and I finished my coffee. Then I showered, found a razor in the cabinet and shaved, dressed, and went downstairs. Marc and Des were at the table sharing the *Globe* and eating Cheerios. Barney was curled under the table looking hungry and hopeful. I poured myself more coffee and sat with them. I lit a cigarette. "Who's got the sports page?" I said.

"Sox lost," said Marc. "I've gotta go back to the police station."

I nodded. "No pitching."

"Fourier called. Wanted me right away. I told him we were up most of the night, give me a break. He said he'd been up all night, too. I told him that was his job. He said he had questions. Sounded ominous. I hope you'll come with me."

"Bullpen, mainly," I said. "They haven't had a decent reliever since Dick Radatz. The Monster. He could mow 'em down. Struck out Mickey Mantle about every time he faced him."

Des had looked up from his paper. His eyes moved from me to Marc and back to me. His face seemed to have acquired new wrinkles overnight. He looked tired and confused.

"Remember Radatz, Des?" I said.

He nodded. "Yes. A large person."

"My father is not a big baseball fan," said Marc. He pushed himself away from the table and then put his hands on it and leaned toward me. "You coming, Brady?"

"I don't do business until I've had two cups of coffee, Marc. It's one of my rules. I don't have many rules. This rule I don't violate." I lifted my mug and peered into it. "Half gone. Or half full. Take your pick. Meantime we talk baseball."

Marc rolled his eyes and sat down. "Speaking of base-ball," he said, "I didn't kill Maggie and they think I did, and I want to get this straightened out as soon as I can."

"Sparky Lyle," I said. "They traded him to the Yan-kees. For the immortal Danny Cater."

"I remember that one," said Des, smiling.

"Jesus Christ," breathed Marc.

Des frowned. "Watch your language, please."

Marc muttered, "Sorry," and lapsed into silence.

I downed the rest of my coffee, wiped my mouth on the back of my hand, and stood up. I took my cigarette to the sink and doused it under the faucet. "Now. Let's do some business."

We said good-bye to Des and went outside. A very large man—he looked as big as Dick Radatz himself—was leaning against my car. He was straddling an old-fashioned balloon tire bicycle. He wore plaid Bermuda shorts and a checked short-sleeved shirt. He sported a black crew cut and a couple days' growth of heavy beard. There was something askew with his eyes.

"Hi, M-M-Marc," he said. His voice was oddly high-pitched. Saliva bubbled in the corners of his mouth as he struggled to pronounce Marc's name.

"Snooker," said Marc. "What the hell do you want?"

"Can Barney come out to play?" said the man after several false starts. When he tried to speak he closed his eyes tight and chewed his lips. Even when he got the words out, it sounded as if he had a mouthful of school paste. I guessed his chronological age at thirty-five. His mental age was difficult to determine.

"Get away from the car," said Marc. To me he said, "The local retard. Pain in the ass."

"B-B-Barney?" repeated the man.

Marc sighed. "The doggie can't come out to play now. He's sleeping. Get your bike off the car. You'll scratch it."

"It's okay," I said. I approached the man and extended my hand. "Brady Coyne," I said.

He nearly tumbled over as he reached to shake. "Snooker Lynch, sir," he stammered.

"Pleased to meet you, Mr. Lynch."

"Can Barney come out?" he said to me.

"Come on, Brady," said Marc.

"How 'bout M-M-Maggie?" Snooker Lynch's eyes appealed to me.

"God damn it, she's dead," said Marc.

Snooker turned to look at Marc. He frowned menacingly at him. "Don't be mean to Snooker," he squeaked. Then his eyes filled with tears. He looked back at me, his eyebrows raised. I nodded.

Snooker spun his bike around. "You're a son of a bitch, Marc Winter," he sputtered. "You're not, sir," he added, to me, I assumed. Then he hopped on his bike and pedaled furiously away.

Marc and I got into my car. I backed out onto High Street and headed east. "You weren't particularly kind to him," I observed mildly.

Marc sighed. "Yeah. It's hard to be patient with Snooker. I feel sorry for the poor shit. But he won't leave you alone. Used to come by to visit Maggie. I used to tease her. Told her Snooker had a thing for her. She'd just laugh. She said she liked him. Understood him. That was Maggie. Loved animals and retards."

Marc directed me to the Newburyport police station. It was a square old brick building near the corner of a one-way street by the waterfront. Several windows on the first floor were barred. A sign indicated that the district court was housed in the same building.

We parked in the lot across the street. I admired the general refurbishing several of the old warehouses had undergone in that part of the city. They had been converted into offices and condominiums and fashionable shops. Sidewalks and vacant lots had been bricked over. Shade trees and benches were scattered here and there for the comfort of the busy shopper and tourist. Good places to lap ice cream cones and recover the energies needed to buy more things and take more photographs. From where we sat we could gaze upon the boats moored in the shelter of the Merrimack near the Route 1 bridge.

We crossed the street and went into the stationhouse. The door opened into a dark, narrow corridor. On the left was a thick window. Behind it a policeman sat at a switchboard. Marc gave him his name and the door to the left past the window buzzed open. A moment later a heavy man with thinning dark hair appeared. He wore a white short-sleeved shirt with a plain blue necktie snug to his throat. Sweat stains the size of basketballs ringed his armpits. His neck bulged over the collar. He glanced at me, then turned to Marc and nodded. "Come on with me," he said, and turned. Marc and I followed him.

He wedged himself into a chair behind a littered desk in the corner of a large room where several other desks sat in a random pattern. Most of them were piled high with folders and envelopes. Three or four of them were occupied by shirt-sleeved cops. They were talking in low voices into telephones wedged against their necks. They ignored us.

"You his lawyer?" said the big man.

I nodded. "Brady Coyne."

"Fourier," he said without offering his hand. He rummaged through the litter on top of his desk, held up a sugar-covered cruller, shrugged, and bit into it. Then he came up with a manila envelope and tapped the corner of it on his desk. "I just got preliminary results from the M.E.," he mumbled around a mouthful. "He examined the body. Hasn't cut it yet. Interested?" He addressed Marc.

"Not really," said Marc. "I know she's dead."

"Gonna tell you anyway." Fourier cleared his throat, glanced at me, then returned his gaze to Marc. He stared hard at him as he spoke. "Apparent cause of death three blows to the skull with a blunt instrument. One across the forehead, one across the bridge of the nose, one along the left side of the head. Each one from a slightly different angle. The weapon was not recovered. Something cylindrical, a bit over an inch in diameter. Possibly a pipe. Or a very heavy piece of wood. The lab will be able to figure it out. Probably tossed overboard after it was used." Fourier arched his eyebrows at Marc, who shook his head back and forth slowly.

"I didn't do it," he said softly. "I liked Maggie. We had no problem."

"Any one of the three blows could've killed her. There is no evidence that she tried to fend them off. No bruises on her hands or arms. They were delivered with great force. Each one smashed her skull like it was an eggshell. Drove splinters of bone into her brain." The matter-of-fact tone Fourier used made it seem even more awful than it was. I suspected he knew that.

"Is this necessary?" I said.

Fourier looked placidly at me. "She was this man's wife. I figured he had a right to know."

"It's all right," said Marc. "I saw her. What I saw was worse than anything he could say."

"She had no clothes on," continued the cop. He picked up the cruller and then put it back down. "The M.E. figures she was sleeping in the berth on your boat. The killer went down and hit her. She sprawled. He hit her again. She fell out of the berth. Then he hit her again. With great force. He used his right hand."

"We had a priest on board," said Marc.

Fourier looked sharply at him. "A priest?"

"Yeah. A small club. Like a miniature baseball bat. We

used it to conk bluefish on the head when we caught them. Can't unhook them when they're alive. Bite your hand off."

"I never heard the term."

"You should see if the priest is still there. It should be hanging by a thong."

Fourier nodded and made a note on a pad of paper on his desk. "Very helpful," he murmured. He tapped the manila envelope. "Another thing the M.E. found out. Your wife had sexual intercourse within a couple hours of her death. You make love to her last night?"

Marc shook his head. "No."

"Who did?"

Marc shrugged. "I don't know."

"She have a boyfriend?"

"Was she raped?"

"The M.E. says no."

"I guess she had a boyfriend, then."

"But, of course, you have no idea who it might've been."

"No."

"Do you have a girlfriend?"

"I don't see—"

Fourier held up his hand. "Sorry. I keep forgetting. You're the grieving husband."

Marc glanced at me. I returned his glance with a frown. He gave me an imperceptible shake of his head.

"You have questions for Mr. Winter?" I said to the policeman. "The man has lost his wife. He's here voluntarily. The least you can do is be civil."

He smiled. It was without humor. "So sorry. Yes, I do have questions." He cleared his throat, stared at the ceiling for a moment, then said, "Tell me again why you went to the boat last night."

"I was home," said Marc with a sigh. "I heard thunder. Thought maybe the boat wasn't secure. So I went to the marina to check her out. Saw the hatch was open and the light on. So I went aboard and saw Maggie. Her body."

"Then what?"

"Then I went to the phone and called you guys."

"The phone at the marina."

"Yes."

"Where did you go before that?"

Marc frowned. "What do you mean?"

"Between the time you saw her and called, where did you go?"

"Nowhere."

"Marc," said Fourier slowly, "we've known each other for a while."

Marc shrugged.

"Not what you'd call friends, maybe. But not enemies, either."

"So?"

"So I'm going to ask you again. Where did you go before you called the station last night?"

"Nowhere."

Fourier sighed and shook his head. He looked at me. "Your client is not telling the truth."

I turned to Marc. "Listen—"

"I'm telling the truth, Brady."

"Supposing I told you that somebody saw you drive up in your truck, park beside the marina, get out and go directly to the telephone."

"I'd say they were mistaken."

"Supposing I had a sworn statement?"

Marc shrugged. "I'd still say they were wrong."

"It seems like a dumb thing to lie about," said the cop.

"I agree," said Marc.

"Let me ask you this, then. Why were you all dressed up if you were in bed and then decided to go down to your boat? I mean, why not throw on a pair of jeans and a T-shirt, instead of fancy pants and a sport coat?"

Marc lifted his eyebrows at me. I shrugged. "It's what was on the chair," he said. "What I had been wearing."

"Look," I said. "If Marc is a suspect here—if you intend to arrest him—then I'm going to advise him not to answer any more questions, since you have neglected to read him his rights. If he's not a suspect, then I think you better develop a different line of questioning."

Fourier stared blandly at me for a moment. Then he gave me another one of his mirthless smiles. "You're right, Mr. Coyne. Nice to have a lawyer here to remind me of my job. What I need to know from your client is who might've killed his wife. See, we don't have a suspect. Now, Marc, here, he's not a suspect. On the other hand, he could become one, if you follow me. I'm not jumping to conclusions or anything like that. Somebody beat in the skull of this young woman. Plenty of malice aforethought, it would appear. So who had the malice? No evidence that there was a scuffle, argument, anything like that. Looks like the young woman went onto the boat, had sex, fell asleep, and whoever screwed her smashed in her head. If it wasn't Mr. Winter, here, then I'm hoping he can help us figure out who."

Marc shrugged. "I don't know. I have no idea. People liked Maggie."

"Evidently she was having an affair," said Fourier.

"Evidently."

"Sex makes for strong feelings."

"I guess."

Fourier puffed out his cheeks and blew out a sigh. "You told me last night she used to work at the Night Owl."

"She did. Maybe it was someone she knew from there."

Fourier nodded. "We're working on it. You must be able to give us a name."

"I can't," said Marc.

"Even a first name would help."

"Maggie never mentioned anybody. I never asked."

"That's unusual."

Marc shrugged.

"What about her family?"

"I don't know anything about her family."

"Parents? Brothers, sisters, ex-husbands?"

"I don't know."

"You expect me to believe you were married to her and she never talked about her family?"

"She ran away from home when she was young. She was a survivor. She had no family. Except me." Marc's hands tightened into fists on top of the desk. "Look. I don't care what you believe. You think just because I did time I must've killed Maggie, and I'm telling you what I know, and you think I'm lying." He turned to me. "Do I have to take this, Brady?"

Just then Fourier's phone rang. He picked it up. "Fourier," he growled into the receiver. He listened for several moments, then said, "Okay." He hung up and pushed his chair back and looked from me to Marc. "That's it for now. We'll be in touch. Meantime, try to remember if maybe, in the shock of events and all, maybe you didn't drive away after you found the body, then change your mind and go back to the marina to make your call, huh?"

Marc stood up. "I'll work on it."

Fourier hoisted himself up from his chair. He looked from Marc to me. "Well, thanks, then." He started us moving toward the door, and when he saw that we were headed in the right direction he returned to his desk. As we left, I saw that he was back in his seat talking into the telephone. He was waving his sugar-covered cruller around in the air to emphasize the points he was trying to make.

We sat in my car, looking toward the river. I started it up and got the air-conditioning blowing hard. The summer sun was high and hot.

"He doesn't believe you," I said after I got a cigarette lit.

Marc was staring off toward the river. "Fuck him."

"Terrific attitude. Might be better if you tried cooperating with the police. They're trying to figure out who killed your wife, remember?"

"Oh, they've got it all figured out."

"Look," I said. "You're a logical suspect. You were there. You've certainly got a motive, if Maggie was having an affair with some guy."

"That wasn't a motive for me."

"Most folks wouldn't understand that."

"Anyway, I am cooperating. I talked to them last night. I talked to them this morning. I told them everything I know."

"You don't seem to know a hell of a lot about your wife."

He shrugged.

I cracked the car window and snapped out the cigarette butt. "You ready to go? I've got to get back to my office."

"Yeah. In a minute," said Marc. He turned in his seat to face me. "What was all that about me driving away and going back? I mean, what if I did?"

"Did you?"

He shook his head quickly.

"Because if you did, then don't you see? You could've killed Maggie, driven away to change your clothes. They would've been bloodstained probably. Then you could have gone back to make the call as if you hadn't been there before. See, if you parked and went directly to the phone, you wouldn't've had any way of knowing she was dead unless you'd been there before."

"You think he has a witness?"

I looked sharply at him. "Could he?"

Marc gazed out the side window. "Yeah. Maybe he could."

"You mean you did drive away and then go back?"

"Yeah."

"If you're serious, then I am about to sign off of this case," I said slowly. "You better tell me why you lied in there, and why you've been lying to me, and what really happened. And you better think carefully before you tell me. If you killed Maggie, I promise you that your best move is to tell me all about it."

"You're pissed, aren't you?"

"You're damn right I'm pissed."

"I didn't kill her."

"It keeps getting harder to accept your word on that."

"Listen," said Marc earnestly. "Here's what happened. After my father went to bed last night, I went out. Met a girl. She's married, okay? I called her, she said she could get out. I met her on a side road in Salisbury, across the river. We talked for a while. Nice girl. Got two little kids at home. Her husband doesn't treat her very well. One thing led to another. We decided to go to the boat." He turned to look at me. "We thought we might go for a little ride. Anchor somewhere."

"Go on."

"If her old man found out she was with me he'd beat the crap out of her. Their marriage is very rocky. She— she might lose her children if he knew she was fooling around. He'd do that. It would kill her."

"She's your alibi."

"Yeah. But I don't want her involved."

"It makes it look bad for you."

He shrugged. "Fourier's got nothing. I'll take my chances. If I have to, okay, I'll tell about her. So we went to the boat. Like I said, the hatch was open. I found Maggie, just the way I said. I told Andy not to come down. We went back to the truck and I drove her to her car. Then I went back and made the phone call."

"And this is the truth?"

"Swear to God."

I thought about it. Unless Marc was arrested, I saw no good purpose to be served by involving this other woman. Her only function in the case would be to clear Marc.

If Marc was now telling me the truth.

"I want to talk to her," I said.

"It won't do any good. She's too scared. She won't tell you anything."

"I'm not a cop."

"It won't matter. I told her not to tell anybody. I told her she wouldn't have to. I told her I'd keep her out of it."

"Fourier is getting ready to arrest you. You realize that?"

"I don't care. I don't want Andy involved."

"Then," I said, "you can count me out."

He was silent for a minute. I lit another cigarette and waited.

"Why do you want to talk to her?" he said finally.

"So I'll know I can trust you."

"You won't tell the cops?"

"If she can corroborate your story, I won't tell anybody until you or she says it's okay."

He frowned at me for a minute, then nodded his head. "Okay. Her name is Andy. Andrea. Andrea Pavelich. She waitresses noons at Michael's."

"Where's that?"

He pointed out the window. "Right around the corner. We could walk there from here."

I put the car into gear and pulled out of the parking lot. "We'll drive. You'll stay in the car while I go in."

"So I won't get to her first, right?"

I grinned. "Right."

5

MICHAEL'S RESTAURANT was housed in a rambling weathered building, once painted white, perched on the edge of the river practically in the shadow of the Route 1 bridge. Windows that looked out on an assortment of pleasure and work boats walled the downstairs dining room. It was nearly empty, awaiting the noontime lunch crowd.

Although I had eaten no breakfast, I had no appetite. The two cups of coffee sloshed acidly in my stomach. I climbed up on a stool at the small bar adjacent to the dining room and looked around. I saw no bartender.

After a moment someone touched my shoulder. "Sorry, sir. The bar isn't open."

She was elderly and gray and dressed in a short blue skirt and yellow jersey, both of which were a couple sizes too small for her. A little plaque over her left breast indicated that her name was Maureen.

"All I want is coffee."

"You can take a table."

I shrugged and spun down from the barstool. She led me to a small table by the window. "Just coffee?"

I nodded. "Is Andy here?"

"Yes. She just came on. She's in the kitchen."

"Would you mind telling her I'm here, like to talk to her?"

She cocked her head at me. "Who're you?"

"Tell her I'm a friend of Marc."

Maureen frowned. "Oh, well, sure."

"Don't bother with cream. I take my coffee black."

She bobbed her head and left. I stared out at the boats. A white-bearded man wearing a long-billed cap and chest-high rubber waders wrestled what looked like a tub of bait aboard a broad-beamed fishing boat. A pair of teenagers lugged fishing gear onto a Boston Whaler. Gulls played musical chairs atop the pilings.

"Maureen said you were looking for me?"

I looked up. Her lower lip was tucked apprehensively under her top teeth. Her hair, the color of Georgia clay, was twisted into a crude bun and secured with a pair of wooden pegs that looked like chopsticks. Her uniform matched the one Maureen wore, except it fit her better.

"Andy?"

She nodded cautiously.

"Can you sit for a minute?"

She shrugged and took the seat across from me. "Who're you, anyway?" She tried to smile. It came up short.

"I'm Marc Winter's lawyer. Brady Coyne."

She narrowed her eyes. "So?"

"I'd like to ask you a couple questions."

"You got proof?"

"What?"

"That you're a lawyer, I mean?"

I reached into my wallet and extracted one of my business cards. I handed it across the table to her. She studied it and then looked up at me. "What do you want?"

"I want to help Marc. He's in a little trouble."

She sighed and shrugged. "I'm not—"

At that moment Maureen returned with a mug of coffee. She placed it in front of me. "You said no cream, right?"

"Right. Thanks."

"You want something, hon?" she said to Andy.

"Uh uh."

After Maureen left, I leaned toward Andy. "I don't want you to be concerned about this. Whatever you tell me is confidential. Do you understand?"

She frowned and nodded.

"Marc and I just came from the police station."

Andy's eyes brimmed with tears. "Please," she said softly.

"Marc hasn't been accused of anything. I just need to know what happened last night. It's very important."

"He promised me," she said. A tear leaked out of one of her eyes. It dribbled down her cheek. She ignored it. "He said he wouldn't say anything about me. Us."

"He didn't tell the police. But he did tell me you were with him."

"He shouldn'ta. It's not fair. We had a deal."

"He explained why he wanted you kept out of it." I lit a cigarette and held the Winston pack to her. She shook her head impatiently. "Will you tell me what happened last night?"

"I'd rather not."

"It would be better for you to tell me than the police."

She looked out the window. She had clear, translucent skin and a little turned-up nose lightly salted with pale freckles. Except for the worry lines etched like a pair of parentheses around her mouth, she looked young and pretty. "I just want to forget the whole thing. Marc and everything. It wasn't worth it." She turned to face me. Now the tears came more freely. She brushed impatiently at them with the back of her hand. "See, my life is a mess. I shoulda just left it at that. Now it's . . ." Her voice faded. She turned again to gaze out the window.

I sipped my coffee and waited. She shook her head slowly.

"Okay," she said to the boats. She looked back to me. "Okay. He called me last night. I was—"

"About what time was that?"

"Nine thirty, maybe?"

"Go on."

"The kids were in bed. My—my husband was out. As usual. Which didn't make me unhappy, believe me. Except I dread when he comes home. See—never mind. Anyhow, Marc said he could come over. I said no. I couldn't—didn't want to do that anymore. He said I shouldn't worry. He said he needed me. He just wanted to see me for an hour. He's real sweet. Marc, I mean. Not Al. Anyway, I said, well, okay. It's—Marc makes me feel good, see. Makes me kinda feel all melty when he talks to me. So different from Al. Oh, I shouldn't be telling you any of this. I don't even know you."

I reached across the table to touch her wrist. "There was a murder last night," I said gently.

"Yeah. I know." She frowned at me. "You don't think Marc did it, do you?"

"He says he didn't."

"Well, he didn't. At least not when he was with me."

"Which was—?"

"Like I said, maybe nine thirty, quarter to ten—"

"You said he called you at nine thirty."

She squeezed her eyes shut for a moment. "Yeah, right. I was watching something on TV and he called during the commercial. Okay. I met him, I guess it was nearer to ten. I checked the kids, made sure they were okay. Told the oldest one, my little girl—she's nine, real responsible—I told her I had to go out for a little while. I locked up and drove down by the beach. It's where we usually meet. I mean, not that I do this a whole lot. But Marc can't exactly come to the house. Anyway, it's maybe ten, fifteen minutes from my house. I had to wait maybe five minutes before he got there."

She stopped and dropped her eyes.

"Go on, Andy."

"What do you want me to tell you?"

"I don't want details of your personal life. Were you with Marc for the rest of the evening?"

She nodded. "Yes. We can't go anyplace. Not like a restaurant or the movies or anything. I just can't take the chance that somebody'll see us. We got out and walked on the beach for a while. Took off our shoes and squished our toes in the sand. Then—"

"You went to his boat?"

She nodded. "He said no one would see us. We could take it out, be alone."

"Did you go anywhere before you went to the boat?"

"No. We drove straight to it. Left my car on the side of the road by the beach."

"What was Marc wearing?"

She cocked her head at me. "What difference is it?"

"Can you remember?"

"Slacks. Sport coat." She shrugged.

"You're sure of that?"

"Sure I'm sure. It wasn't that long ago, you know."

"So you went to the boat."

She widened her eyes. "Oh, wow. He didn't want me to see her, but I did. I was right behind him, and when he saw her lying there he sort of jumped back and like gasped and I could see her over his shoulder. I've never seen anything . . ." She hunched her shoulders and pressed her forearms together in front of her.

"Do you have any idea what time you arrived at the boat?"

She hugged herself. "Midnight, maybe. I don't know. Maybe a little later. It was maybe one o'clock when I finally got home. Marc drove me back to my car. Told me not to say anything, he'd take care of it. I mean, he knows if Al ever found out. Oh, jeez, he'd kill me. Or worse. Luckily Al wasn't there. I went to bed. Hardly slept at all. I pretended to be asleep when Al came pounding in. Drunk. So what else is new, huh?"

"What time did Al get home?"

She shrugged elaborately. "What time does he ever get in? When he feels like it. It must've been after two. Him and his buddies." She snorted through her nose. "I had to wake him up before I left to come here. Told him to take care of the kids so I could go make a few bucks to feed them."

"Did Marc mention a name when he saw Maggie? Her body, I mean?"

"I don't getcha."

"As if he had an idea of who might've hurt her."

She shook her head. "No. I mean, I don't think so. It was so scary and weird I'm not sure I'd remember."

"Can you think of anything you didn't tell me, Andy?"

"Like what?"

"I don't know. Anything Marc might've said before you got to the boat. Or when he drove you back to your car."

She squinted at me. "I know what you're thinking, Mr. Coyne."

"You're one step ahead of me, then."

She smiled quickly. "You think Marc killed Maggie and then called me up so he could pretend to find her body. Then I'd be his whatchacallit, his alibi. Right?"

"The thought occurred to me, yes."

"Well, he'd have to of killed her before nine thirty. They can figure that out, can't they?"

"I think so. I'll check."

"Look. I mean, I'm worried for Marc's sake and all that. But I gotta tell you, I'm more worried about me. You seem like a nice guy. You make me feel like I can trust you." She shook her head slowly. "If I can't—I mean, if you're going to tell people what I just told you— you gotta know that I'm like dead. Really."

"They haven't arrested Marc. I suppose they may suspect him. But I know that Marc doesn't want you involved. If he didn't do it, then they'll have no evidence that would justify their arresting him. In which case, he won't need you."

She nodded. "And if he did do it, then I won't be able to help him anyway."

I knew it wasn't that simple, but I saw no point in adding to this young woman's problems. "That's about it," I said. I extracted a dollar bill from my wallet and put it at my place at the table. Then I pushed myself back and stood up. "We both have to get to work. I appreciate your honesty." I held my hand to her.

She grasped it. "I told you the truth. I really did. I just hope . . ."

"Don't worry."

"I mean, if it comes to it, I'd have to say what happened. I realize that. It would only wreck my life." She tried to smile. "What the hell. It's a mess already."

On my way out of the restaurant I had to step over the outthrust ankles of a big blond guy who was leaning back with his elbows propped on the bar. He made no effort to move, and as I went past him I could sense his eyes following me. When I stepped outside from the dim interior of the restaurant into the bright noonday sunshine, I paused to squint. A voice behind me said, "So whadda ya think you're up to, pal?"

I turned. It was the blond man. He wore a grease-spotted T-shirt that stretched taut across his chest. It failed to meet the belt of his jeans, revealing an expanse of pink hairless flab. His beefy face was red. His little pig eyes slitted narrowly. The side of his mouth turned down in an ugly sneer.

I looked him up and down. "What's it to you?" Lightning quick with the wisecrack. That's me.

"You hittin' on my old lady in there. I wanna know who the fuck you are."

"My name is Coyne, sir," I said, realizing that this was Andy's husband, Al, and my responsibility was to protect her. "I sell insurance. Disability insurance. Everybody who works should have disability insurance. It's important for restaurant personnel. All sorts of accidents can befall a restaurant employee. Disability insurance is especially important for unsalaried workers. You," I added, smiling at him, "should have disability insurance. Do you have a good plan, sir?"

"I don't need no disa-fuckin'-bility insurance, friend, and neither does my wife."

"Oh, everybody does. You sure I can't interest you—?"

I saw it coming, a straight-armed club with a fist the size of a cantaloupe on the end of it. My brain gauged distance and velocity and instructed my body to dodge and my chin to tuck under the protection of my shoulder. Al's blow exploded high on the side of my head, and as I staggered and fell backwards, I thought sadly how when I was younger I could have slipped that crude, amateur attack.

Instinctively I rolled into a fetal position. He kicked wildly at me, but I was moving and he missed. He fell on me, flailing with the sides of his fists. I tried to rise onto hands and knees but his body pressed on me, slippery with our mingled sweat. His breath against my face reeked of last night's beer and offended as much as his prodding and gouging knees and elbows.

Abruptly his weight was off me. I pushed myself into a sitting position. My breath burned in my lungs. Damn cigarettes.

Marc had his forearm levered across Al's throat. The big guy stood there panting. "Lemme at the bassard," he rasped.

"Take it easy, Al," said Marc. "You got a problem with this man?"

"He was hittin' on Andy. Nobody hits on Andy."

"I was just trying to sell her insurance," I said quickly, to clue in Marc. "Mr. Winter here is going to buy some."

"That's right," said Marc. "This man is an insurance salesman."

"I don't fuckin' believe that," muttered Al. But his mouth screwed up stupidly, as if the concept was difficult for him.

I stood up and held out my hand to Al. "Hey, no hard feelings, sir," I said. "Little misunderstanding."

Al jerked himself out of Marc's grasp and stood there, bulging arms hanging, his big chest heaving. "I was watchin' this sombitch in there," he said, looking at me but talking to Marc. "No fuckin' way he was sellin' insurance. I'm gonna find out what the hell's goin' on. The tramp's gonna pay."

"Come on," I said. "Shake my hand."

Al turned his head and spat. It landed beside my foot. "I ain't stupid," he muttered, and turned and lumbered away.

Marc and I watched him go. He climbed into a rusted old pickup with wood two-by-tens for bumpers. It started up with a roar, spewing a great cloud of exhaust, and spun its wheels in the gravel as it left.

"You better tell Andy what happened," I said to Marc

after Al's truck had left. "Make sure she keeps the story straight."

He nodded. "Al'll beat the shit out of her anyhow."

"I told him I was trying to sell her insurance."

"He doesn't believe that. He didn't believe you, he won't believe her."

"We're stuck with the story. It's the best I could do under the circumstances."

Marc shrugged. "The gals in the restaurant all know Al. They'll cover for her. I'll be right back."

Marc went inside. I went over to my car. I leaned against it and gingerly touched my skull. I discovered a small tender lump where Al's fist had connected with what was, fortunately, a glancing blow on thick bone. I found a small tear on the left knee of my pants. My shirt was dirty. Otherwise I seemed to be none the worse for the experience.

Once upon a time I could handle myself. I played sports. I was quick and strong. I had my share of brawls. I was gifted with quick reflexes, limber muscles, an instinct for self-defense. But this time, I realized, I had been lucky. Al was fat and slow and unskilled. Yet had not Marc interceded I could have been hurt badly. The years had eroded my athlete's graces, leaving, I had to admit, an out-of-condition middle-aged man at the mercy of bullies like Al.

Yale Law School did not teach us the gentleman's arts. There had been times during my practice of the law when I felt it was an inexcusable omission.

Marc returned. "I told her. She's petrified of the guy. But she'll stick to the story. You tried to sell her insurance. She told you she wasn't interested. Still," he added, "you ought to be careful. Al's not a guy to fool around with."

"Ah, he's not so tough."

Marc cocked his head and examined me. He grinned. "It's all relative."

"You probably should take care yourself."

He nodded.

We got into the car and headed back to Des's house. "Andy corroborated your story," I said.

Marc nodded. "Of course she did."

"You've put her into a tough spot."

"I didn't know Maggie was going to get killed," he said softly.

I pulled into Des's driveway. Marc got out of the car and then leaned in. "Why don't you come in, get yourself cleaned up?"

"Good idea."

Des was seated at the kitchen table eating a sandwich and watching a little portable television. When Marc and I went in, he looked up. "My word! What happened to you?"

"I had a disagreement with a gentleman on insurance," I said. "Not everybody believes in the importance of insurance."

"You should act your age, Brady," said Des mildly, and returned his attention to the television.

I climbed the stairs to one of the upstairs bathrooms. I found myself favoring my right leg, the one with the bum knee. In the mirror I saw where the skin had been scraped off my cheekbone. I took off my shirt and doused my face and chest with water. "Act your age," I said to my reflection. "Good advice," my reflection replied.

I went back downstairs. Des offered me a sandwich, but I declined. "Getting beat up always ruins my appetite," I said. "Anyway, I've got to get back to the office."

I told Marc to let me know if the police summoned him again, said good-bye, and went out to my car. Des followed me. "I've got to know," he said to me.

"I don't think Marc did it, if that's what you mean."

He nodded. "I thought I was prepared for anything. I mean, after Connie left . . ."

I put my hand on his shoulder. "If Marc was with you until nine thirty last night—"

"I went to bed around nine. Marc was here then."

"Then he's in the clear."

"He was with a woman, wasn't he?"

I nodded.

Des shook his head. "If only Connie . . ."

"If only my uncle had steel wheels," I said, "he'd be a choo-choo train."

Des nodded doubtfully. I slid into my BMW and pointed it at Copley Square.

6

JULIE WAS HUNCHED OVER the computer processing words when I got to the office. She looked up when I walked in, frowned, returned her attention to her keyboard for a few beats, and then did an exaggerated double take.

"Oh, *sir!*" she said. She leaped to her feet and made a swooping curtsey. "So *wonderful* of you to grace us with your presence. Welcome to our humble law office."

"Julie, cut the shit, will you? I got about three hours of sleep last night and I'm in no mood."

"Several of your clients are in no mood, also." She glared at me out of the corners of her eyes and returned to her seat. "You got a bunch of messages on your desk, if you feel like looking at them."

"I am prepared to get to work," I harrumphed.

"Don't strain yourself."

I pivoted and strode toward my inner office.

"Looks like the truck won," called Julie.

I stopped and touched the abrasion on my cheek. "It was a draw."

I detoured to Mr. Coffee, poured myself a mug, and

took it into my sanctum. Julie had left a pad of yellow legal paper in the precise center of my otherwise clear desk. I eased into my chair, lit a Winston, sipped my coffee, and read the list of phone messages she had noted for me.

First were the weekend calls from the machine:

Dr. Adams, Friday P.M., regretting missing you, wondering about your banker's hours, to try you at home.

Nathan Greenberg, Sunday, 3:00 P.M., will try again Monday first thing. Urgent, quote-unquote. Did not identify himself further.

Unidentified woman, sultry voice, claiming wrong number. I doubt it.

Next Julie listed the calls she had taken during my absence in the morning:

Dr. Adams again, wanting to report on fishing trip and make you jealous. No need to return call.

Mr. Paradise, calling from pay phone. Cautions extreme secrecy.

Mr. McDevitt, wanting lunch. Has new joke. Refuses to share with me.

Mr. Ellard. Massachusetts Bar. Your professional association, not the joint around the corner. Reminding you of your article on trusts vis a vis new tax laws. I told him it was in the mail. I'm typing it now.

Ms. Winter. No message.

I picked up the pad and took it back out to the reception area. Julie had the computer clicking like a muted Western Union telegraph. I touched the back of her neck. She turned her head and looked up at me without missing a beat.

"Take a break," I said.

"Can't. Your article is late."

"How's it sound?"

"I'm typing it, not reading it."

"Oh."

"Actually, I fixed it up. It's pretty boring, but at least it's now in proper English. Your spelling wobbles."

"Of course it's boring. It's supposed to be."

She stopped typing, sighed, and swiveled around. I placed my hands on the front of her shoulders, bent, and kissed her forehead. "Sorry I was late. Sorry I didn't call."

She shrugged. "It's what I expect."

"Come on. Lighten up, kid."

She smiled. "If I didn't pout, you'd be upset."

"True."

"Were you really in a fight?"

"I was attacked by a cowardly bully."

"The lady's husband?"

"Actually, yes. But it's not what you think."

She grinned. "Sure."

"Tell me about these calls," I said.

She took the pad from me and squinted at it. "Not much to add."

"Who's this Greenberg?"

"Don't know. He didn't identify himself."

"Did he call back?"

She frowned. "No. He said he would. He was very emphatic about it, actually. Said he'd call early and keep trying until he got through."

"Well, I guess he changed his mind. You told Charlie McDevitt to forget about lunch?"

"I told him I hadn't heard from you, didn't know when or if you'd be in."

"Doc Adams?"

"He started to tell me about largemouth brown trout or something."

"Bass? Largemouth bass? There's no such thing as largemouth brown trout, Julie. You fish for brown trout with dry flies or nymphs on rivers like the Deerfield. Now, your largemouth bass—"

Julie crossed her eyes. "You can't expect me to keep your fish straight. I have enough trouble with your girlfriends."

"The fish are much more important," I said. "Did Doc say where he went?"

She rolled her eyes. "I don't remember."

"Come on, Julie. This is important."

"For crying out loud, Brady."

I held up my hands, a gesture of surrender. "Okay, okay. What about Frank Paradise?"

She smiled. "As usual. Refused to say his name. Assumes our phone is tapped or something. Tried to talk in code. He's getting real paranoid, Brady."

"He's always been real paranoid. He's probably invented something new, watching out for the pirates. What'd Kat Winter want?"

Julie's mouth tightened in disapproval. "Oh, she's so charming. Said it was personal, not professional. Somehow, the way she used the word 'personal' . . ." Julie made her voice low and sultry in imitation.

"She's a client, Julie. Not to mention the fact that I spent the wee hours last night with her father and brother in Newburyport."

"Ah," she said. "A day of fishing on the high seas and an evening of drinking beer and talking theology. No wonder you're late."

"Marc's wife was killed last night."

Julie stared at me. After a moment, she said, "You're not kidding, are you?"

"No."

"You really know how to smack a girl between the eyes, Brady Coyne."

"I would've told you. But you were so damn grouchy I said the hell with it."

"What happened?"

I shrugged. "I'm not sure. The police suspect Marc, of course. He's in the clear, though, I think."

"How is Mr. Winter doing?"

"Des? Des is okay, I guess. He seems perceptibly older each time I see him. I think he was fond of Maggie. He appeared more confused than anything. Flustered. As if God were playing dirty tricks on him."

"I like him."

"Me too. He's had more than his share of troubles."

"So all these phone calls," she said. "I guess, by comparison, they're not that important."

"To the people who made them they are. This is what we have to keep in mind."

She nodded. "I wasn't the one wandering into the office at one in the afternoon."

"When you get that article done, why don't you take off the rest of the day?"

"Can't. I've got responsibilities."

I shrugged. "Don't say I didn't suggest it."

I went back into my office, pulled out a phone book, and tapped out the number for the Newburyport police. The guy on the switchboard put me through to Detective Fourier. "Fourier," he said, not unpleasantly. "Can I help you?"

"It's Brady Coyne. I was in this morning with Marc Winter."

"Yeah. How you doin'?"

"Okay. Look. I need some information."

"Yeah?"

"You've got the medical examiner's report. What's it say about the time of death?"

He hesitated. "That's police business, Mr. Coyne."

"Oh, come off it."

"I don't talk about cases with citizens."

"I'm hardly a citizen. I'm a lawyer. We're in the same business. Marc Winter's in the middle of this thing."

"He's a witness, that's all. For now. You and he've got no rights."

"I'm not talking about rights. I'm talking about professional courtesy."

I heard him laugh quickly. "You want courtesy, Counselor, you came to the wrong place. You want courtesy, try this. Fuck off."

"Now listen—"

He had hung up on me. I replaced the receiver on its cradle and said, "Up yours."

I swiveled around in my chair and stared out at the smoggy Boston skyline. I couldn't fathom Fourier's refusal to talk with me. He had been relatively forthcoming only a few hours earlier in his office. I just needed a simple piece of information. If Maggie had died after ten o'clock on Sunday night, and if Andy Pavelich had told me the truth—and I believed she had—then Marc's innocence seemed certain. If Maggie had died earlier than that, given Des's vagueness, then I had to question whether Marc was using Andy for an alibi.

Fourier had called Marc a witness. "For now," he had added. It was logical to suspect Marc. He had cited a witness who saw Marc pull up in his truck and go directly to the pay phone at the marina. Okay. None of that excused his refusal to cooperate with me.

I rotated my chair back to my desk and pecked out the number to the state police headquarters on Commonwealth Avenue. The receptionist transferred me to

Inspector Horowitz's secretary, who remembered me and switched me to Horowitz himself.

"Ah, Coyne," he said cautiously. "I infer a request for a favor."

An explosion sounded in my ear. "You still hooked on Bazooka?" I said.

"I'm chewing gum, yeah."

"You better cut back. You'll contract a case of TMJ."

"I'm trying cigarettes. Whenever I get the urge to chew, I smoke a cigarette. It's not working, though. I can't shake the gum habit."

"It's a bitch. Look. You're right. I need a favor." I outlined the Marc Winter case for him. "I figure the state cops are involved somehow. Fourier's shutting me out."

"That's his prerogative."

"All I need is the girl's time of death to nail down Marc's innocence. No reason he can't help me out."

"You tell him you've got a witness for Winter?"

"I'm trying to avoid involving the girl. For obvious reasons."

Horowitz popped a bubble. "So this is just to satisfy your own mind."

"Right."

"You want to buy me lunch some time?"

"You got it."

"I'll get back to you."

We disconnected. I leaned back and laced my hands behind my head. There came a scratching on my door. "Come on in," I called.

Julie opened the door. "The light went off your phone. Got a minute?"

"For you? Always."

She took the chair beside my desk and placed a sheaf of papers in front of me. "Your masterpiece. Want to look it over before I send it out?"

I waved my hand. "No. It's boring."

"I made some changes."

"Thanks. I trust you."

She shrugged and reached for the papers. I put my hand on her wrist. "You're looking especially beautiful today," I said. "I like your hair that way." It was true. Julie had clear, pale skin and shiny black hair. She was letting it grow. It fell in loose folds, framing her face and accenting her cheekbones.

She turned her face away and looked at me from under hooded lids. "Okay. What do you want?"

"Want? *Moi?*"

"Come off it, Counselor."

"You got me wrong, kid."

"Sure."

I grinned at her. "I want you to see if you can figure out who this Nathan Greenberg is."

"Oh. Is that all?"

I shrugged. "Shouldn't be that hard. Try the phone books."

"Oh, right. Simple. Supposing the guy's from Florida or L.A. or something?"

"More likely he's local, right?"

She frowned, and then she said, "I suppose so. He just didn't sound . . ."

"Jewish?"

She shrugged. "I guess."

"Jeez, Julie."

"You really want me to try to get him, huh?"

"I'm curious," I said. "He said it was urgent, he'd call first thing, then nothing."

"The man changed his mind, right?"

I shrugged. "So humor me."

She twirled around and went to the door. When she got it opened she turned. "You have any idea how many Greenbergs there must be?"

"Lots, I'll bet."

"Or how many Nathans?"

"I appreciate it."

She closed the door behind her, somewhat more forcefully than was necessary. Julie and I sometimes got confused over our respective roles. Sometimes I actually acted as if I were the boss.

She usually found a way of setting me straight.

I made a few phone calls. Charlie McDevitt was out to lunch. Shirley, his secretary, told me about her new granddaughter. I expressed awe that she could be a grandmother. She told me this was number nine. I guessed she had been a child bride. She giggled.

I caught Kat Winter between appointments. "It was nice to see you," she said.

"Ditto."

"So tell me. Did my darling brother do in his wife?"

"I'm pretty sure he didn't."

She was silent for a moment. "I wish I could believe that."

"Marc's not a murderer, Kat."

"You know him so well." She laughed quickly. "Anyway, Brady. I hope you'll take Daddy fishing one day soon. He's not going to handle this thing too well."

"I should be able to shake loose later in the week."

"Try to arrange it so we can have dinner. Swordfish's fresh at the Grog."

I promised to try.

Doc Adams was at the hospital repairing a cleft palate. Susan Petri, his unbearably sexy assistant, told me he wouldn't be back to the office. I wondered how Doc ever got anything done around there, with Susan slinking around to distract him, or how his wife, Mary, tolerated it. Something solid in that marriage.

So much for returning my phone calls. I glanced at my watch. A little after three. I realized I hadn't eaten all day. My stomach had passed the point of hunger. A vague nausea had set in. I went over to the mini refrigerator in the corner and took out a can of Pepsi. A little jolt of sugar and caffeine would straighten me out.

My phone buzzed. I sat at my desk and picked it up. "Mr. Horowitz is on line two," said Julie. "Look, Brady. There are two columns of Greenbergs just in the Boston directory. Seven Nathans, plus two with N for an initial."

"So call 'em up."

She sighed. "I haven't even looked in the suburban books."

"Whatever you can do."

"Take line two."

I hit the button. "What'd you come up with?" I said to Horowitz.

"Time of death," he said without preliminary, "estimated between ten and one. See, they take the body temperature, factor it in with the environmental temperature, compute the loss. They examine the stomach contents, and if they know when the deceased ate last—"

"I know about this stuff," I said.

"—add in lividity. That's—"

"Yeah. How gravity pools the blood when it stops circulating."

Horowitz paused. "Anyway. Between ten P.M. and one A.M. That's what they came up with."

"She hadn't been dead that long when Marc found her, then."

"If you want to trust this estimate," said Horowitz. "Forensic pathology's not a very precise science. Even when they do it right. Which they don't always do, you know."

"I wish you wouldn't shatter my illusions that way."

"Hey," he said. "One of the pleasures of my life, shattering illusions. Especially yours." I heard him chuckle softly. "More to the point," he continued, "the police will take this estimate—what the M.E. very candidly calls an estimate, and what everyone knows is crude at best—and they'll convert it into rigorous fact. If you were at the scene of the crime at five minutes of ten holding a bloody bludgeon, you're clear. Because the thing had to've happened after that. If you've got an alibi starting at ten-oh-five, tough shit. You're a suspect. That's how cops think."

"Which would seem to clear Marc."

"Assuming his girlfriend is telling the truth, and everybody's got their times straight."

"I assume those things."

"The Newburyport cops don't know those things. The Newburyport police don't even know about the girl. If there was a girl."

"Oh, there was a girl."

"And if she was telling you the truth."

"I felt she was," I said lamely.

Horowitz snapped his gum. "Before ten, after ten. That's all they'll care about." I heard the rustling of papers. "I talked with our officer on the case, who's real intrigued by one thing."

"I'm not going to have to beg you, am I?"

"You're buying me lunch, I'm helping you out." He cleared his throat. "It's the sperm they found in the girl. It seems to explain things."

"Sure," I said. "It gives Marc his motive. Cheating wife. Tried and true motive. He suspects she's fooling around. Follows her to the boat, waits for her paramour to show up, listens while they murmur and moan and cry out in ecstasy, getting more and more pissed off, waits for the guy to leave, goes aboard, confronts Maggie. They argue. She makes reference to his diminished masculinity. Taunts him. Tells him she's got a million lovers. He calls her a slut. Whatever. He loses it. Clobbers her. She dies. So he leaves. Changes his clothes. Goes back and calls the cops."

"Except for this girl you say can alibi him."

"Right. Fourier doesn't know about her. So, okay. After Marc kills Maggie, he calls Andy Pavelich, goes to meet her, brings her back to the boat and pretends to discover the body. Takes his date home, goes back to the marina and calls the cops."

"That would fit," said Horowitz.

"Except for the times."

"Those estimates are crude."

"There's something else, too, of course."

"Sure—"

"The guy who screwed Maggie," I said.

"Naturally. That guy could've whacked her. Problem is—"

"They don't know who that guy is. And they do know who Marc is. Bird in the hand."

"Cops tend to think that way," said Horowitz.

"Well, what does your investigator say? They going to arrest Marc?"

"Our investigator doesn't say anything. Fourier's the one who's on Winter's case. They've got nothing but circumstance. They can't place your client there at the alleged time of death. No weapon. No certifiable motive. Supposition, that's really all they've got. Still," he added, "it doesn't look good. There is this witness who saw Winter drive up and go directly to the telephone. Neat sort of case, actually. Real nice suspect. Possible motives up the ying yang." Horowitz sounded a bit nostalgic, as if he wished it were his case.

"You got a name for that witness?"

Horowitz paused. I heard papers riffle. "Nope."

"What do you make of that?"

"Anonymous tip. Unreliable witness. Vague on description. Drunk, maybe. Hard to say."

"Well, listen. I appreciate it," I said.

"Oh, you'll pay."

"Willingly."

"So what're you going to do?"

"Me? I'm going home, have a bowl of Lipton's chicken noodle soup and go to bed. I feel cruddy."

"About your client, I mean."

"Nothing. He hasn't been accused of anything."

"That's what I'd do, too."

I watched the first three innings of the Red Sox game. It was six to one, Baltimore. Hurst was wild. I snapped off the television and went out onto the little balcony that clings to the side of my apartment building. I snuffled in a few lungfuls of sea air. From my perspective six stories up in the air, Boston Harbor lay tranquil before me. A ferry, carrying a load of pleasure seekers on an aimless, alcoholic cruise of the harbor islands, scrolled a white wake across the sea's moonlit surface. The sounds of a rock band echoed up to me. In the harbor's murky depths, I knew, all sorts of foul chemicals were busy reacting with each other. Deadly bacteria mutating like crazy. Fish gasping and dying. Mollusks growing fat on the poisons.

The patch of Atlantic Ocean in front of me had recently been proclaimed the dirtiest in the land. Considering all that, it didn't smell so bad.

I went back inside, brushed my teeth, dropped my clothes onto the floor, and crawled naked between the sheets. I picked up my tattered copy of *Moby-Dick* and opened it to a random page. Excellent bedtime reading. It never failed to make my eyelids droop.

The phone beside the bed jangled. This was getting to be a habit. I picked it up.

"This is Coyne," I said.

I heard a series of staccato grunts, like a chain saw that was reluctant to start.

"Hello?" I said. "Who is this?"

There was a moment of silence. Then a high-pitched voice stammered, "Eyesore maybe swisher ballman."

"Excuse me? I didn't understand—"

I heard a click.

I wondered what Snooker Lynch had been trying to say to me.

7

I SCRIBBLED the syllables, as well as I could phonetically work them out, into the inside cover of *Moby-Dick:*

Eyesore maybe swisher ballman.

I looked at it and added a couple question marks.

It must have been Snooker Lynch, the retarded guy who had been leaning on my car in Des Winter's driveway, though I wouldn't have thought Snooker would know how to use a telephone, never mind look up my number in the book. Hard to know how much significance to place on anything that Snooker Lynch might tell me, even if I knew what he was trying to say.

I put Melville's tome back onto the bedside table and flicked off the light. My eyelids clanged shut.

I awoke, as usual, before I wanted to. I pulled on a pair of sweat pants and shuffled barefoot to the kitchen. Beyond the expanse of glass of the sliders, I could see that a heavy cloudbank had cruised in overnight and settled over the harbor. It hadn't yet started to rain.

I loaded up the electric coffee machine and retrieved

the morning *Globe* from outside my door. I tossed it onto the kitchen table and retreated to the bathroom, where I showered and shaved. By the time I had donned my office clothes, my coffee was ready. I poured a mugful and took it and my newspaper out onto the balcony.

I found Maggie's story in the Metro section on page twenty-seven under the headline NORTH SHORE WOMAN CLUBBED TO DEATH.

> The body of a Newburyport woman was found aboard a pleasure craft moored in the Merrimack River early Monday morning by local police. She had apparently been killed by repeated blows to her head with a heavy clublike object.
>
> According to police spokesman, Newburyport Detective John Fourier, the dead woman has been identified as Margaret Winter, wife of Marcus Winter of Newburyport.
>
> "At this stage of the investigation," said Fourier in a prepared statement, "we have arrested no one. We are cooperating fully with the state police."
>
> Fourier indicated that the police are pursuing several promising leads.

Dozens of trees had been slain to provide enough paper for all the words that had been written about the bones in Bill Walton's feet. Barrels of ink had been consumed in printing the stories about an obscure tendon in Oil Can Boyd's pitching arm.

Maggie's death got four short paragraphs.

For Des's sake, I was glad it was short and obscure and made no mention of his connection to her.

Another story on the page facing the piece on Maggie caught my eye. SLAIN ATTORNEY IDENTIFIED, it read.

> The body of a man found stabbed to death in a Danvers motel Monday has been identified as Nathan R. Greenberg.

Greenberg, 43, was an attorney from Asheville, North Carolina.

Bernard Tabor, manager of the Sleepytime Motel in Danvers, told reporters that he became suspicious when a Do Not Disturb sign remained on Greenberg's door after checkout time on Monday. "Finally," said Tabor, "I unlocked the door. It was about one in the afternoon. There was blood all over the place, and this little bald guy is lying there on the bed with no clothes on and he sure looked dead to me. But I knew enough not to touch anything. I called the police."

Danvers police indicate that Greenberg died of multiple stab wounds. They are seeking for questioning a woman who allegedly visited the victim in the evening.

Julie had observed that there were a lot of Greenbergs in the phone book, several of them named Nathan. She called them all. None admitted to calling my answering machine on Sunday.

Here was another Nathan Greenberg. This one was from North Carolina. He wouldn't have been in any of the phone books Julie used. He had been a lawyer. He could have called me on Sunday and left a message on my machine. He probably couldn't have called me on Monday. He was dead on Monday.

In a motel in Danvers.

Which lies very close to Newburyport.

I reread the story. Something bothered me about it. I couldn't put my finger on it.

I pondered it as I ate a cold wedge of leftover pepperoni and sausage pizza and drank a big glass of orange juice for breakfast.

I tried to figure it out as I drove from my apartment to my office in Copley Square.

When I sat at my desk, I read the story again.

The motel owner referred to Greenberg as a "little

bald guy." I reread the phrase. Bald guy. Bald man. *Ballman.*

Eyesore maybe swisher ballman.

What could a person who talked as if he had a mouthful of congealed oatmeal be trying to say that would come out sounding like that?

Something about a bald man, I was willing to bet. And I was further willing to bet the bald man in question, the *ballman* Snooker Lynch tried to tell me about over the telephone, was none other than the dead Nathan Greenberg who, I also believed, was the identical Nathan Greenberg who had tried to contact me.

I wrote Snooker Lynch's verbal burps and grunts, as I had spelled them phonetically, onto a yellow legal pad and stared at them. If *ballman* truly was "bald man," and Snooker's ballman *was* Nathan Greenberg, then I was prepared to believe that Greenberg's death was connected to Maggie's.

I went out to Julie's desk. She was busy at the computer. "Excuse me," I said.

Without turning she said, "Hang on a sec."

She tapped at the keys for another minute or two, then swiveled her head to look up at me. "Yes, my lord?"

"Remember that phone message from Greenberg?"

She nodded.

"You said he didn't sound Jewish, remember?"

"Well, he didn't."

I touched her shoulder. "Don't get huffy. What did he sound like to you?"

She frowned. "He spoke soft. Southern accent, maybe."

"Maybe?"

She shrugged. "He sounded southern, yes."

They sound southern in North Carolina.

I showed her what I had written down from Snooker Lynch's phone conversation. *Eyesore maybe swisher ballman.* She frowned at the words. "What's this, some e. e. cummings poetry or something?"

"It's something a guy who doesn't talk very well said to me. I think the word 'ballman' means bald man. Greenberg was bald."

She shrugged. "So?"

"So I want to try to figure out what the rest of it means. Help me."

We took turns saying the syllables aloud, slurring them, stammering and spitting and substituting similar sounds, trying to reconstruct what Snooker's poor brain had wanted his mouth to say. After a while we gave up on "eyesore" and went to work on "maybe."

"May," said Julie. "Mayney. Mamie. Maisie. Shit."

"It's not shit. Do it alphabetically."

"Maybe. Maycey. Maydie. Mayfee. Maygee. May—"

"Hold it," I said. "Say that again."

"Mayfee? Maygee?"

"That's it!" I kissed her on the cheek, a very wet enthusiastic one. "Maggie. It's Maggie. He was saying something about Maggie and the bald man."

Julie frowned doubtfully. "What about the rest of these words?"

"I'm not sure it's important," I said. "Gotta go make a phone call."

I went back into my office and called Horowitz at state police headquarters.

"Now what?" he said when the switchboard put me through.

"What can you tell me about this guy Greenberg who got killed up in Danvers?"

He coughed. "Why?"

"You smoking?"

"Yeah. No substitute for gum, though. So why do you want to know about the Danvers thing?"

"He was a lawyer. I have a thing about lawyers getting bumped off."

"You want to get smartass, don't ask me to divulge police business to you."

I lit a Winston. "I'm sorry. It's a dumb hunch. I had a call from someone named Nathan Greenberg on Sunday. Then Des Winter's daughter-in-law gets murdered. Then this guy named Nathan Greenberg turns up murdered in Danvers. Danvers is pretty close to Newburyport."

"Dumb hunch is right."

"Pretty please?" I said.

"Jesus," he mumbled. "You won't leave me alone, will you?"

"Never."

He sighed. "Okay. Hang on."

I finished the cigarette. It took him about five minutes, during which time I drew scrolls and arrows on the pad of paper on which I had translated Snooker Lynch's message.

"Doesn't look like this one is related to the Newburyport thing," he said when he came back on the line. "This guy Greenberg was stabbed six times in the throat and chest. The M.E. figures a serrated kitchen knife, though the weapon hasn't been recovered yet. The guy was robbed. No watch. Found his wallet in a trash barrel by the motel parking lot. No cash, no credit cards. They put his time of death between nine Sunday night and three Monday morning. Guy at the motel says he thought he saw a woman go into Greenberg's unit sometime in the evening. Couldn't make any kind of identification, of course, either of her or of the car she was driving. I surmise that broads go in and out of that place all the time."

"Hookers," I said.

"Yeah. My guess is one of them offed Greenberg."

"Any idea what Greenberg was doing in Danvers? In the paper it said he was from North Carolina."

I heard papers rustle. "Nothing on that here. I imagine someone'll look into that, though it doesn't appear relevant."

"It might be if his death and Maggie's are connected."

"I'll pass along your hunches," said Horowitz. I didn't believe him.

"Is that it?"

"Well, he was driving a Hertz rental. Last year's Chevy Citation. Blue. Got it at the airport Saturday. Ah, he works for a firm in Asheville. Slavin, Jones is the name of it. They haven't done an autopsy yet. When they do, I'll let you know whether he ate Chinese or Italian before he got killed." He paused. "And that is all. And I really ain't supposed to tell you, so don't go blabbing about it."

"If you didn't know you could trust me, you wouldn't have told me."

"I just like it better when you owe me than when I owe you."

I thanked Horowitz and hung up.

I swiveled around and stared out my office window at the sky. It was uniformly pale gray, the color of spit, and it hung low so that the tops of the taller buildings looked fuzzy.

The estimated time of Greenberg's death overlapped with Maggie's. It was at least theoretically possible for him to have murdered her and returned to his motel in Danvers, whereupon someone could have murdered him.

Or Maggie could have killed him, sped back to Des's boat, and gotten her head smashed in.

The same person could have killed them both.

Or the two deaths were totally unrelated.

Horowitz clearly leaned toward the latter conclusion. I had to agree that it was the most compelling, especially in the absence of Snooker Lynch's phone call, which, for no particularly good reason, I had decided not to share with Horowitz. All he would have needed to hear from me was that my suspicions had been fired by a series of nonsense sounds from a retarded man over the telephone late at night.

On the other hand, if Snooker *had* seen Maggie with Greenberg . . .

I reached the answering machine at Des's house. I hung up halfway through his recorded invitation for me to leave a message.

A no-nonsense female answered the phone at Kat Winter's office. "Winter, Inc.," she said. "May I help you?"

"I'd like to talk to Kat."

"Miz Winter is in conference just now. May I have her return your call?"

"When did Kat get a secretary?"

"I'm not a secretary, sir. I am an administrative assistant."

"My secretary would rather be called a secretary. I tried to make her an administrative assistant once. She got pissed. Said she was a secretary and proud of it. She runs the damn office."

"Do you want to leave a message, or what?"

"Julie—she's my secretary—says if you're really liberated, you don't get hung up on what you're called. You gotta take pride in your work and make sure you get paid what you're worth for it."

"We're very busy. If you want Kat to call you back, you better leave your name and number. She doesn't pay me to listen to a bunch of bullshit when I answer the phone. She tells me just to hang up if some asshole tries to give me a hard time."

I took a deep breath. "Hey. I'm sorry. I've got things on my mind. My name is Coyne and I'm Kat's lawyer and I do need to speak to her and I apologize for coming on strong. Okay?"

"Hold on a minute, Mr. Coyne. I'll get her for you."

I whistled a few bars from Beethoven's Pastoral Symphony while I waited for Kat to come on the line. When she did, she sounded out of breath.

"Brady, what's up?"

"You been jogging?"

"Actually, I was in the bathroom."

"Your secretary—I'm sorry, administrative assistant—used the same euphemism Julie uses. Conference. She said you were in conference."

"You probably bring the sports page with you."

"Enough scatology for one day. Simple question. I tried to call your father or Marc, but they're out."

"Arranging things for Maggie, I think."

"My question is this. Do you know how I can get ahold of Snooker Lynch?"

"Snooker? Why in the world would you want to do that?"

"He tried to call me."

"Snooker?"

"I think so."

She laughed. "I wouldn't've said he knew how to use a telephone. How do you know Snooker?"

"I met him yesterday outside Des's house. He was on his bike, leaning against my car."

"He lives with his aunt down near the river. Far as I know it's just the two of them."

"Do you know her name?"

"Sure. Dotty McCarthy. She used to work in the town hall. Retired a few years ago."

"You wouldn't mind looking up her phone number, would you?"

"I wouldn't mind, but I happen to know it's unlisted. She got too many crank calls. People making fun of Snooker. It's so easy to set him off, they could just say something to him on the phone and they'd start to hear things breaking and poor Snooker snarffling and gurgling, trying to swear and having no luck at it. So Dotty got her number changed, took it out of the book. Snooker's kind of an institution around town. Like everybody's pet. But there's always a few Neanderthals who love nothing better than to pick on someone like Snooker."

I sighed. "So can you tell me how to find Dotty McCarthy's house then?"

She chuckled. "Sure, I can tell you. You going to pay a visit?"

"Looks like it."

"Today?"

"Yes."

I jotted down the directions Kat gave me. I was familiar enough with the area. It wasn't far from the marina where Des moored *Constance.*

"Got it," I said when she was done.

"Supper with me after your visit, then. I accept no excuse."

"The Grog at six thirty."

"You got it."

"Give my best to your, um, administrative assistant."

"I'd rather save your best for myself."

I spent the morning signing all the stuff Julie gave me to sign, talking to the people she got on the phone for me, and conferring with the one client with whom I had an appointment, a periodontist named Barton who sported thick gold necklaces and copper bracelets and a three handicap. Rick Barton had earned lots of money cutting and stitching rich people's gums, none of which he was inclined to share with the government, and he had ignored my advice by retaining a tax accountant who promised more than he could deliver.

I told Rick I doubted we could avoid steep penalties, but that I might be able to keep him out of prison. This seemed to make him happy. He invited me to play the member-guest with him at his country club in Concord. I snapped my fingers in disappointment, citing a fictional court commitment.

I went out at one and brought back Italian subs from across the street. Julie and I spread waxed paper over her desk and ate together, licking oil and bits of onion and hot pepper off our fingers, sipping Pepsi, and talking baseball. She felt that seven and a half games was not too far from first place in the middle of July, and that the Red Sox were poised for a big run at the old gonfalon.

Julie actually talked that way. The old gonfalon.

"They've got some good sticks riding the pine," she said.

Also, she pointed out that the shortstop had been throwing a lot of leather recently.

I told Julie I was looking forward to the football season. "The Pats're going to abandon the I formation. Mix it up. Go to the shotgun, even on first down. They've strengthened themselves at cornerback, and the linemen are learning their stunts. Question is Miami. They still can't even beat the spread down there, even though they don't play in the Orange Bowl anymore."

Julie picked up a chunk of provolone and dropped it into her upturned mouth. She looked like a baby bird at feeding time. "You football nuts talk funny," she grumbled.

It was about three o'clock when I pulled into Dotty McCarthy's side yard. She lived in a shoebox-shaped little house. The mustard-colored paint was cracking and peeling. A rusty rotary lawnmower sat in the middle of the front yard, where it had either died or run out of gas halfway through its job. Half of the grass stood about six inches high. The unmowed half was about a foot of shaggy grass and weed. A few white wildflowers bloomed in the uncut part.

I mounted the crumbling cement stoop and tried the bell. I detected no ding from inside. I depressed it again, waited, and then knocked. After a moment I thought I heard movement inside. I knocked again.

The door opened suddenly and completely. "Now you just leave the boy alone!" snapped the woman from behind the screen door. She was shaped like a light bulb, with a small head, narrow shoulders and chest, and massive hips that seemed to span the doorway. Her hands were resting on those great pillow hips. A half-smoked cigarette protruded from the precise middle of her mouth. An inch of ash clung precariously to its tip.

"Mrs. McCarthy?" I said, using my Yale Law School smile.

She narrowed her eyes. "You're not who I thought you'd be," she said. It did not come out as an apology.

Without touching her cigarette with her fingers, she sucked on it. The ash fell onto her chest. She brushed it away.

"I'd like to talk to your nephew."

"Why?"

"He called me last night. I wanted to be sure I understood what he said."

"So who're you?"

"I'm a lawyer," I said. I took out my wallet, extracted one of my business cards, and held it up in front of the screen door for her to see.

She turned her face away. "Ain't got my glasses on. That could say you were the President himself, wouldn't impress me. What'd you say your name was?"

"Coyne. Brady Coyne."

She frowned. "Yup. That's what he was sayin'.

Sounded more like 'bone.' He was sayin' he gotta call Mr. Bone."

"That was me. Coyne. He was trying to tell me something. I think it might've been important, but I couldn't understand all of it."

"Nobody understands what Ernest says. Except me, of course. But then, I've known him a long time. Twenty years, nearly, he's been with me." She cocked her head. "Most folks don't even bother tryin'. They figure his brain's no good and he ain't got anything worth listenin' to. You figure different, huh?"

"Yes. He was trying to tell me something."

She cocked her head and looked at me differently, as if she had suddenly noticed something for the first time. Then, evidently satisfied that she had seen it accurately, she nodded. "His brain ain't quite right, of course. But it works. For some things, it works good. If he could talk right, folks wouldn't tease him so. He ain't as dumb as he seems, I can tell you that."

"Well, I know he can use a telephone."

"He can use lots of things."

"They have special schools, new therapeutic techniques, you know. The Commonwealth is very enlightened about diseases like his."

She shrugged. "I reckon it's too late now. Maybe when he was a boy . . ."

"They have good programs for adults."

She shrugged, and I guessed Dotty McCarthy liked things exactly the way they were.

"Is Snooker—Ernest—at home?"

"Nope. Hardly ever is, 'cept at mealtime. I feed the boy good. Three times regular. Eats like an elephant, I don't mind telling you. Takes all my pension just to feed him. Otherwise he's off on that bicycle of his, lookin' for people to pay attention to him. Fact that some of them tease and taunt him don't seem to matter. He don't know the difference. Mostly, people are nice enough. The boy just likes company. You look down on the docks. He likes to hang around the boats, talk to the people there. Might find him dangling a handline off the end, tide's right. Sometimes he'll bring home some flounder or mackerel, proud as a kitten with a dead mouse. I cook 'em up for us. About what the poor boy's good for. Bringing home dead fish. Blessed shame."

Dotty McCarthy had made no move to invite me in. I could hear the murmur of television voices coming from somewhere in the darkened interior of her house. It was becoming disconcerting talking through a screen door.

"Does your nephew stay out late at night?" I asked the woman.

She pushed the door open a crack and snapped the cigarette butt past my ear out into the yard. "Usually," she said after a hesitation so long that I thought she was going to ignore my question.

"What about Sunday night?"

She frowned. "Today's what?"

"Tuesday."

"Let's see. He was in last night. We watched television some. I went to bed usual time. He stayed up. Agitated, he was. That when he called you up?"

I nodded. "Last night, yes. Late."

"Okay, then. Sunday." She bobbed her head up and down. "The night that woman got herself killed, right?"

"Yes."

"He was out most of the night. Up early the next day, too. Ate breakfast and took right off on his bike."

He had pedaled straight to Des's house, I figured, where he was waiting when Marc and I came out.

Dotty McCarthy was leaning back, as if to listen to what was happening on her television. I took the hint and thanked her. I turned to leave.

8

I PARKED beside a rusted dumpster in the gravel lot on the opposite side from the silver-shingled shack that was the marina's office. I noticed a pay phone on the outside wall, the one from which Marc Winter had called the police the night he found Maggie's bludgeoned body. An orange-painted steel mesh walkway led out across one hundred feet of sparse-growing marshgrass to the complex of floating docks where the boats were moored.

I once asked Des why they didn't construct a nice boardwalk to replace the esthetically offensive steel gridwork. "Ecology," he said. "Can't keep the sun off the vegetation. It'd disrupt the delicate balance of things." Des pointed down at the sere grass that sprouted up around the beer cans, empty potato chip bags, and discarded bait containers. "The brainstorm of some desk jockey in Washington, no doubt."

The marina was constructed like a T that had been crossed a dozen times. I guessed that fifty boats were moored there. Bertrams, Egg Harbors, Grady-Whites, Makos, and Chris-Crafts, serious ocean-going vessels for serious fishermen, along with Boston Whalers and ballis-tic-shaped speedboats and a variety of sloops and yawls. *Constance,* Des's Bertram, was moored in her usual slip, I noticed. There seemed to be no sawhorses or signs or ribbons to indicate that she was out of bounds. The po-lice, evidently, had completed their forensic research on her.

Snooker Lynch was crouched at the very end of the long central pier. His bicycle lay beside him, its handle-bars upturned, its front wheel cockeyed, so that it looked like a huge wounded insect. I approached him quietly. He sat on the edge, dangling his legs. A plastic bucket and a cardboard container like the kind for leftover chow mein sat on the dock beside him. The latter con-tained his bait, I guessed.

His body was arched tensely forward. He held the line in his fingers like a flute, his wrists cocked delicately beside his ear as if he might hear the nibble of a fish. I stood behind him for a minute without disturbing him. I lit a cigarette. He sat as still and rigid as a statue. The wooden dock rolled rhythmically under my feet. The tide was pushing upriver. It was good to fish the incom-ing tide, I knew.

I coughed and said, "Mr. Lynch?"

He swiveled his head very slowly and peered at me for a moment. Then he returned his attention to his line. I moved forward and sat beside him.

"How are they biting?"

He shook his head without looking at me.

"I want you to tell me about the man you saw with Maggie."

He shook his head again.

"Did that man kill her?"

He twitched the line he was holding, pretending, I figured, to be more interested in the fishing than our conversation.

"Did she kill him, then?"

He hauled in his line with an awkward hand-over-hand motion. His hook and the one-ounce oval lead sinker came in festooned with seaweed. He plucked it off with the patience of an old woman undoing a mistake in her needlepoint. When he had cleaned off the hook, he reached into the cardboard container and plucked out a sandworm, an ugly lizardlike creature with cruel pincers and lots of legs. He placed it on the dock beside him, produced a knife from a sheath at his hip, and sliced the critter neatly in half. Both halves writhed and wriggled. He picked up one half and deposited it in the Chinese food container. The other half he impaled on his hook, which he lowered between his legs into the river. The line made an upstream arc as the accelerating tide bowed it.

Without looking at me, Snooker began to make sounds, a series of false starts that I had the sense not to interrupt. Finally he came out with "Wone talka please," which I understood to mean that he wouldn't talk to the police. It was amazing how much easier he was to understand face to face than over the telephone.

"I'm not asking you to talk to the police. But please tell me what you saw."

His fingers gently strummed and plucked his fishline. "You shook my hand," he managed finally to say. Then he said, "You called me mister."

He lapsed into silence, as if that had explained everything. I flipped my cigarette butt into the water. It meant that he would talk to me, because I had extended him the simple everyday courtesy I'd extend to any man. It also suggested that, at one time in his life, he had tried to talk to the police, earning a ruder response.

"I spoke with your aunt," I said to him. I took my cue from him, not looking at him, but studying the river that flowed the wrong way in front of us. "She thought I might find you here."

"Going to catch supper for her," he sputtered. It came out, "Gonkitch sufferer."

"She's very nice. She told me your name was Ernest. Do you prefer to be called Ernest?"

"Snooker's okay."

I lit another cigarette. I tapped him on the shoulder, and when he turned I held the Winston pack to him. He frowned and shook his head. "Cancer," he said, this word pronounced very clearly.

"You're right," I said, and he smiled.

"Eyesore maybe swisher ballman," he said. Except this time it was clear to me what he was saying. "I saw Maggie with the bald man."

I waited, and after a few minutes he began to talk. Sunday afternoon he had been pedaling down High Street. As he passed Des Winter's house, he noticed a car stopped in front, its motor running. Maggie was standing by the window on the driver's side, leaning down, evidently giving directions. The driver, said Snooker, was bald.

That night he went to the marina to fish. He had just started to push his bicycle over the steel mesh walkway when headlights shone behind him. He turned to look, and when he did he recognized Marc Winter's pickup. He saw Marc get out of his truck and go to the pay phone by the marina office. "Numba biz," said Snooker, shaking his head. None of his business. He continued on his way to the end of the pier and began fishing. A few minutes later police cars began to pull up. He ignored them. But a cop wearing a suit approached him and began to question him. "Furry," said Snooker. Fourier. Snooker told Fourier what he had seen. The policeman, I inferred from the new anger that accompanied Snooker's sputters and grunts, had prodded and cross-examined him to the point where he refused to say any more.

I guessed that he had perfected the trick of acting stupider than I figured he really was. His speech impediment did not necessarily denote a brain impediment of the same magnitude. Snooker was smart enough, all right. Smart enough at least to know when it was better to let others think he was dumb. In any case, Fourier gave up and left him alone.

The next afternoon he overheard talk in town about Nathan Greenberg's murder in nearby Danvers. To Snooker, Greenberg wasn't *a* bald man. He was *the* bald man. So he called me. Because I was probably the only person who had recently treated him like a man rather than an imbecile.

It was a long shot that Greenberg was the same bald man Maggie had given directions to the day they both were killed.

"What kind of car was the bald man driving?" I asked Snooker.

"Blue Citation," he replied promptly, although what he said didn't sound exactly like that.

"Are you sure?"

He frowned and the corners of his mouth turned down. He looked as if he might cry.

I touched his arm. "You must know your cars," I said quickly.

He nodded vigorously. I hoped I hadn't lost him.

"And what did the man look like?"

"Ballman. No hair."

"None at all?"

Snooker grinned wetly. "Nonatall."

"Was he wearing glasses?"

He shook his head.

"Beard or mustache?"

"Nonatall," he said proudly, as if he had learned a new word.

He suddenly ducked his head forward. His fingers caressed the fishline as if he were stroking a woman. With a grunt he jerked the line upward. A moment later he dragged in a fish. It looked like a gray rubber football that had been run over by a truck. A flounder. Snooker unhooked it tenderly and dropped it into his bucket. He rebaited and lowered his line.

I stood up. "Looks like they're starting to bite. I'll be on my way."

He turned and looked up. Then he smiled. He wiped his hand across the front of his shirt and held it to me. I shook it. "Thanks for your help, Mr. Lynch," I said. He nodded and turned back to his line.

It was a little past five thirty when I got to the Grog. Both the downstairs and the upstairs bars were full, the after-work crowd, the majority businessmen in suits with vests, the rest young women clustered in protective pairs and trios. I took a table in the back section of the downstairs dining room and ordered a bourbon old-fashioned. Then I went to the pay phone and put through a credit card call to Horowitz.

When he came on the line, I said, "One more thing."

"You're a pest, Coyne."

"Thank you. You don't happen to still have the stuff on the Greenberg murder on your desk, do you?"

I heard him sigh. "Been keeping it here, all excited that you might call me back."

"Great. Tell me again what kind of car he was driving, then."

"I'm too tired even to ask why." He ruffled some papers. "Chevy Citation. Blue. Hertz rental. I think I already told you this."

"You did, yes. And Greenberg himself. Just how bald was he?"

"Jesus," muttered Horowitz. "I got a photo here. Bald. Very bald. Completely bald, actually. Hard to tell, but maybe he shaved his skull."

"Mustache or beard?"

"Eyebrows're about it in the hair department."

"Did Greenberg wear glasses?"

He paused. Then he said, "Nothing about glasses here. They didn't find any glasses."

"Thanks," I said.

"Hey, wait."

"What?"

"You going to tell me what this is all about?"

"I think Maggie Winter and Nathan Greenberg knew each other."

"You think?"

"For now, that's it, yeah. I think."

"You'll keep me posted?"

"I'll share every one of my dumb hunches with you."

He blew a bubble and popped it loudly in the telephone. "You better," he said.

Kat showed up at twenty after six. She was wearing a pale flowered silky dress, sleeveless and scoop-necked. It showed off her silvery-blond hair and light, buttery tan.

She slid into the seat across from me and grinned. "What're we drinking? I'm parched."

"I'm starting my second old-fashioned. You're early."

She flapped her eyebrows like Groucho Marx. "I just couldn't wait."

The waitress appeared. Kat ordered a gin and tonic. Then she said to me, "You're on your second drink, you've been here a while. You must be very excited."

I shrugged elaborately. "Nowhere else to go, that's all."

"A man of steel." She reached across the table and rested her fingers on top of my hand. Her nails scratched my skin lightly. "Mr. Unseductable, huh?"

"That's me." I turned my palm up and held her hand for a moment before she smiled and gently pulled it away. "How's Des doing?" I asked.

Her eyes clouded. "Not that good, like I told you on the phone. He's—I think this is reminding him of—you know, what happened . . ."

"Your mother," I prompted.

She nodded. "Anyway, Daddy liked Maggie. I suspect she and my—they were a lot alike at that age or something. Living with Marc doesn't help him. I mean, after all . . ."

"You still believe Marc is responsible?"

The waitress appeared and placed Kat's gin and tonic on the table in front of her. Kat looked up and smiled quickly and brilliantly, an actress's trick, a meaningless but utterly persuasive smile in the middle of her disturbing thought, like being able to nod your head up and down while saying no.

Kat's smile faded as instantly as it had appeared. "Oh, he's responsible, all right," she said. "I'm not saying Marc did it. But there's something. He knows something."

She tilted up her glass and took a long swig. When she lowered the drink she smiled at me and shrugged. "Anyway," she said, "enough of that. I'm famished. What'll we have?"

We ordered blackened swordfish and a bottle of chilled Chardonnay, which we consumed rapidly to cool our overheated tongues. As we ate, I told Kat what I had learned from my talk with Andrea Pavelich, who confirmed Marc's alibi, and my encounter with big Al Pavelich in the parking lot outside Michael's restaurant afterwards.

"He beat you up?" she said, grinning.

"He threw a sucker punch. I wasn't ready for it. I didn't have a fair chance to defend myself."

"She said she was with my brother, though, huh?"

I nodded. "I believed her."

"But she won't tell the police?"

"She's afraid. Marc is trying to protect her. From Al."

Kat sipped her wine. "Understandable. Especially if she's not telling the truth."

"Well, I think she is," I said, and Kat shrugged.

I told Kat about Snooker Lynch's late-night phone call and my visit with him at the marina and the suspicions I was harboring about a connection between Maggie and Nathan Greenberg.

"We didn't really know anything about Maggie," mused Kat. "I don't think Marc did, either. Suddenly she was there, in the middle of our lives, as if she had just been born full grown, with no history, no family, no connections. But of course, she had them. Connections, history, I mean. Maybe this guy Greenberg was part of that."

"Maybe he killed her," I said.

"But why?"

I shrugged.

"Maybe Marc killed them both," she said. "Who knows?"

"I want to know," I said.

"Why?"

I laughed away the question. "Why not?"

"Like the mountain, right? It's there, might as well climb it. Is that it?"

"Oh, I'm sure my motives are more complex than that," I intoned with mock solemnity.

"What the Freudians call displacement and sublimation."

"The Freudians make it all into sex."

She grinned. "Isn't it, though?"

We lingered over coffee. Kat had landed a new account, a developer who was renovating an old warehouse on the waterfront and wanted to market the units as office condominiums. She hoped I'd help her with the contract. She was thinking of expanding, taking on an artist and a copywriter to free herself up to do what she believed she did best, which was to solicit new accounts and plan ad campaigns. I assured her I could help her work out the details.

I walked her to where she had left her car. The breeze off the waterfront carried moisture which glistened in Kat's hair when we passed under the streetlights.

When we arrived at her Saab, she fumbled in her purse for her keys. She unlocked the door and then turned to lean back against it. "Suppose I can't talk you into coming over for a nightcap," she said.

"Nope. Tired. Thanks."

She brushed a strand of hair away from her forehead. "Didn't think so. What I'd really like . . ."

"What would you really like?"

She cocked her head for a moment, then shook it. "Nah. Forget it."

"Come on. What?"

"Would you take me fishing?"

"You?"

"What, I'm a girl?"

I shrugged. "I didn't know you were interested in fishing."

"What I want to do is stand in the surf and throw those big plugs way out there like those macho men do. Can't women do that?"

"I don't know why not."

"Well?"

I nodded. "Okay. We'll do it sometime."

She put her hands on my hips and held me there, leaning the top half of her body back against the car, her eyes mocking. "Not good enough, fella. You're putting me off. Daddy always did that. Ask him to do something, he'd say, 'maybe,' or 'we'll see,' or, 'sometime.' When, Brady?"

"Soon, okay?"

She laughed. "Not good enough. Tomorrow."

"Jesus, Kat. You are a tough broad. I've been out of the office too much lately."

"After work, then. Say around six."

I calculated. I could break away around four, go back to my apartment and change, and easily get to Newburyport by six. The tide would be coming in, just as it was on this day. The bluefish might be running near the beach.

I could do it. Did I want to do it? I rarely declined a chance to go fishing. I liked teaching tyros how to do it. But there was something about Kat's flirtatious demands that discomforted me. On the other hand, there was something else, too, the way her eyes flashed . . .

"Okay," I said. "Your job is to get the gear organized. Des has it all in the garage. He'll help you put together what we need. I'll meet you there at six. We can go over to Plum Island, try the outer beach."

"Really? You'll really take me?"

"Isn't that what lawyers are for?"

"And you'll teach me how to do it?"

"We'll see how apt you are."

She reached up and put her hands on the tops of my shoulders. "You are a dear man," she said, "and I think you will find me very apt."

Her mouth approached mine as if in slow motion. Her eyes were wide and inquisitive, as if she might retreat if she detected a negative clue in my face. The truth was that her pelvis pressing itself against mine more than counteracted the feeble, if sensible, "no" that came from my brain.

She was Des's daughter, after all. I thought of her as the college kid she had been when I first met her, not this thirty-two-year-old businesswoman. Besides, I preferred my seductions to be mutual and subtle.

But there was her pelvis, and when she kissed me I kissed her right back, and I had the distinct feeling that kissing was an art she had practiced, an exercise more in proficiency than in spontaneous passion. A marketing tool, perhaps.

Proficient, hell. She was truly gifted. Her tongue and her teeth and her lips all embarked on separate but neatly coordinated missions, complementing perfectly the work of her fingers at the back of my neck and that persuasive thrust and roll of her hips.

She slid her mouth away from mine an instant before I would have—another measure of her gift. She stood away from me smiling. She rubbed her mouth with the back of her hand.

"Jesus, Kat."

"Something else lawyers do?"

"Oh, yeah. We are great kissers."

She grinned and had the good sense to refrain from innuendo. She opened the car door and ducked inside. Then she rolled down the window. "Tomorrow at six, then," she said.

"At Des's house."

"You will see just how apt I can be."

9

I LEFT KAT and aimed my BMW for Boston. When a sign announced that I had entered Danvers, I had an idea. So I exited Route 95 in Topsfield and got onto Route 1. I found the Sleepytime Motel on the right. It was almost eleven o'clock. I hoped the same night manager who had discovered Nathan Greenberg's body would be on duty this evening, too.

The motel looked like it had been built during the postwar automobile boom, forty years earlier, when U.S. Route 1 funneled vacationers from Boston and Hartford and even New York City to resorts in Hampton and Ogunquit and Kennebunkport, and truckers steamed up and down the coast, and businesses boomed everywhere. Then along came Interstate 95, all eight lanes of it, and Route 1 was left to the locals and the occasional aimless tourist. The motels and gas stations and ice cream stands that had sprouted along the roadside like goldenrod in the forties and fifties were mostly either boarded up or torn down or converted into shops selling automobile parts and carpet remnants.

The Sleepytime Motel typified that postwar, no-nonsense, put-'em-up-quick-and-cheap school of architecture, a series of plywood boxes joined and stacked in the shape of a shallow angular horseshoe. Twenty-four units, twelve down and twelve up. A red neon sign boasted of waterbeds, telephones, and cable television. Grass grew from cracks in the concrete turnaround. The neon failed to illuminate the L in the word MOTEL on the sign. There was a half-finished swimming pool under construction in front. Judging by the way weeds sprouted from the piles of dirt, that project had been terminated.

I parked outside the office and went in. A pale young man with a short fuzzy haircut was lounging in a swivel chair behind the counter. He wore earphones and was reading a paperback book. My "Hello" failed to capture his attention.

I moved into his peripheral vision and waved my hands. His eyebrows jerked up and he smiled. He turned off the radio in his shirt pocket, closed his book onto his forefinger, plucked off his earphones, and stood up.

"Sorry, sir," he said. "Can I get you a room?"

"Are you Bernard Tabor?"

He frowned. "Yes, sir."

"You were here the night Nathan Greenberg was murdered, then?"

He nodded eagerly. "I found the body. It was me who called the police. They quoted me in the paper."

His paperback was a detective story by Ed McBain. I wondered if crime fiction was a recently acquired taste of his. He leaned his forearms on the counter toward me, eager, it seemed, for an audience.

I lit a cigarette. "I have to go over some questions with you again."

"Boy, you guys are thorough."

I gave him a stern, no-nonsense, official-business glare. "We have to be," I said. He nodded eagerly. He wouldn't ask me for identification. He wanted me to be some sort of official person. He had lucked into a moment of fame and would welcome every chance to milk it.

"Tell me what happened again, Mr. Tabor." Joe Friday had nothing on me. Just the facts.

"Well," he said, "I was on duty from four to midnight Sunday, okay? At midnight we close up, because there's just not that much transient business on Route 1 these days. Not worth keeping a man on duty all night. Mr. Franklin, the day man, he was sick so he asked me to take his place Monday. Yesterday, that is. That's how come I was here in the morning. I'm happy for the work. I mean, it's not that hard, you know? I'm working my way through school, I can use all the money I can get. Mr. Franklin worked today. He was pissed he'd missed all the excitement. Anyway, I came back on at seven yesterday morning. Terry, the girl who cleans the rooms, she comes on at eight. So about eleven thirty she tells me number seven's got the Do Not Disturb sign on the door. Now, I figure the man's still got the girl in there—"

"What girl?"

"Like I told the papers. He had a visitor, oh, maybe nine Sunday night. I didn't check the time. Didn't really think about it. Girls come and go in this place, to tell you the truth. Anyhow, I didn't notice her leave, which doesn't mean she didn't, just that I didn't notice. Or she could've left after I closed the office. But I figured maybe she was still there, or else she stayed late and Mr. Greenberg was sleeping in. You know, not much sleep . . ."

He waggled his eyebrows. I nodded and smiled appreciatively at his suggestion. "What did the girl look like?"

"I didn't really see her. Not so I could describe her. I just happened to glance out the window and saw the car pull up in front of seven. I wasn't paying attention. She got out of the car and went in." He shrugged.

"Did you get a look at the car?"

He shook his head. "My view was blocked by the other cars."

"How do you know it was a woman?"

"She was wearing a dress. I could see her bare legs."

"Color of hair?"

"It was too dark to see." He lifted his hands in a gesture of surrender. "You guys asked me all this already. I'm sorry."

"Okay. Go ahead."

"Anyway, about one Terry came by again. She's all upset, because she still hasn't gotten into seven, and she's done all the rest and she wants to leave. So I went over and knocked on the door. I yelled for Mr. Greenberg. It was completely quiet in there. Thinking back, it was spooky quiet, you know what I mean?"

I nodded.

"At first I figured the guy just forgot to flip the sign around when he left. Then I noticed his car was still there. I knocked again. I had this weird feeling. Last winter some guy had a heart attack in his room, and when they found him he'd been dead for two days. So I unlocked the door. The curtains were closed and it was dark, so it took me a minute before my eyes adjusted. Oh, man! There was blood everywhere. I backed out and told Terry not to go in. Then I called the police."

"You did exactly the right thing," I said.

He pursed his lips. "I had to use some judgment."

"How did Mr. Greenberg pay for his room?"

"Visa card. He took it for three nights."

"Did he make any phone calls from his room?"

"Nope."

If this was the Nathan Greenberg who had tried to call me, he must have called me from a pay phone in Newburyport. It would have been at around the same time Snooker Lynch saw him talking to Maggie in front of Des's house on High Street. Still, it would have been nice to be able to pin it down.

"What about other visitors, Mr. Tabor?"

He shrugged. "Not that I noticed. It's not my business. People rent a room, they can do what they want in it. Most of the people who take rooms here are local, if you catch my drift."

"I catch your drift. Did you talk to Mr. Greenberg at all?"

"Uh uh. Like I said, I came on at four. He had checked in by then and he was gone. I didn't notice when he came back."

"But he was here when the girl came?"

"I assume he was. His car was there. The girl parked beside it."

"But you don't know what she was driving."

"No. She parked on the opposite side of his car from here. Not that I was paying that much attention."

"Is there anything you forgot to tell us before," I said, "that you've remembered since then?"

He shook his head. "I've been over and over it in my head. Wish I could picture that girl. She probably did it, right? Anyhow, I can't. Don't you sometimes—you know —hypnotize important witnesses? Get them to recall something that's in their subconscious?"

"We do that sometimes," I said. "It's a good idea. I'll pass it along."

"I'm happy to help, you know. Anything I can do."

I nodded and held my hand to him. He seized it eagerly. "I appreciate your help, Mr. Tabor. We'll be in touch."

He frowned. "I didn't catch your name, sir."

"Horowitz," I told him. "Detective Horowitz. State police."

He nodded slowly. "I figured you were a state police officer. I just put two and two together."

*   *   *

A female voice dripping cornpone and grits said, "Slavin, Jones" into the phone the next morning.

"I'd like to speak to one of the lawyers," I said.

"This *is* one of the lawyers. It's what we've got here. Lawyers. We're an office plumb full of lawyers. Now, you just tell me what you want, I'll hook you up with the right one. Divorce? Tax? Personal injury? Estate?"

"I'm calling from Boston. About Nathan Greenberg."

"Right," she said, as if she knew it all along. She hesitated. "You'll have to talk to Mr. Slavin, then. He's been handling this."

"I don't care who I talk to," I said, "but I'm not the police."

"Mr. Slavin's already talked to the police."

"All I want to know is why Greenberg was in Boston."

"I'll see if Mr. Slavin will talk to you."

A moment later a man's voice said, "Who is this?"

"My name is Brady Coyne. I'm a lawyer. I'm calling from Boston. I'm inquiring about the Greenberg case."

"Your police have already gone through their motions. What is your interest?" His voice lacked any discernible accent whatsoever.

"It's complicated," I said. "I'm trying to establish a connection between Greenberg's death and the death of a relative of a client of mine."

I heard Slavin sigh. "I spoke with a policeman on the telephone. Greenberg was in Boston for a client. What happened to him does not appear to be related to his business."

"How can you know that?"

Slavin cleared his throat. "I told the police why he was in Boston and what kind of a man he was. It was they who seemed to feel his death was unrelated."

"What did his client want that brought him to Boston?"

"Well, you know I can't tell you that."

"Without your client's permission."

"Technically."

"How might I get your client's permission?"

"I suppose I might ask for it."

"Would you?"

He laughed.

"What's so funny?"

"Your police," he said. "They never asked that."

"What I'd like to do is talk to Greenberg's client."

"It's possible."

"Mr. Slavin," I said, "what kind of man *was* Greenberg?"

"Pardon me?"

"You said you told the police what kind of man he was."

He hesitated. "That's right. I did try to explain this to your police. It's no great secret hereabouts." He cleared his throat. "Let me put it this way, Mr. Coyne. Nathan Greenberg was a pretty fair country lawyer. He didn't mind taking certain kinds of cases. You know, the sorts of cases that others might find, ah, distasteful. But cases that do need to be handled. In fact, he preferred them. For that reason, he was an important member of this firm. But, frankly, he was a rather unpleasant person. Most of us down here are not terribly distressed at his, ah, passing. Shocked, yes. Something like this is always a shock. But our firm will survive. And candidly, we will not miss Nathan Greenberg."

"Can you say more about that?"

"His—well, his attitude toward women, actually."

"Sexually, you mean?"

"Well, really, sir . . ."

"Was he brutal, is that it?"

Slavin said nothing for a long moment. Then he said, "I've already told you more than I should have, Mr. Coyne. I'm sure you understand."

I thanked Slavin and told him to have Greenberg's client call me collect. He said he would, or else he'd get back to me himself.

I tried Horowitz. He wasn't in. I left my number. I tried to call Marc Winter and reached Des. He sounded depressed. Marc was out. Des said he'd ask him to return my call. I tidied up a will. I dictated a couple letters to Julie. Smoked a cigarette. Smoked another one. Called Kat at her office. Kat said she was busy but looked forward to fishing with me. She made it sound like an assignation.

Marc called me back. "Maggie ever mention a guy named Nathan Greenberg?" I asked him.

He hesitated, then said, "Not that I remember."

"This'd be a lawyer from North Carolina."

"Nope. Don't think so. Why?"

"A hunch. Can I ask you something more personal?"

"You can ask."

"Maggie's sexual preferences?"

"Jesus, Brady."

"I mean, was she into sadomasochistic stuff?"

"Chains and leather and whips, you mean?"

"I guess that's what I mean."

"Not with me she wasn't. You think someone smashed in her head because it turned her on?"

"Maybe it turned him on."

"She was healthy, Brady. Innovative, but, you know, conventional. She—"

"Hey," I interrupted. "I don't want any details. You answered my question."

Horowitz returned my call about two thirty. "I thought of pretending I didn't see this message," he said.

"Appreciate it. On Maggie Winter and Nathan Greenberg again."

"How'd I guess?"

"Any chance of talking to whoever's in charge of the cases?"

"Look, Coyne. I have dutifully shared your insights with the two officers, okay? They told me to say thank you very much, they think they can handle it now."

"Did you tell them about the possible link between the two murders?"

"How do I make this clear to you?" Horowitz paused and snapped his gum. "They thought of it all by themselves. They've done almost as much homicide work as you. They think your speculations are interesting. They are even taking a look at the possibility that the Winter woman stuck knives into Greenberg. They have your number. I gave it to them, in the hopes that they might actually call you, so you would stop calling me. I gather that so far this hasn't worked."

"No one has called me."

"Coyne," said Horowitz, "it's not like you and I are big buddies."

"We're not? Jeez. I would've said we were pals."

"Call it what you want. You are becoming a pain in the ass, okay? I mean, I don't want to hurt your feelings. But—"

"You already did."

"If that's what it takes."

"I guess I can take a hint."

"Just call us even," he said. "You don't owe me, I don't owe you."

"But I do. I owe you lunch."

"Forget it. Stop calling me. I will release you from your obligation."

"Fuck you," I said good-naturedly, but he had already hung up on me.

It was getting close to four o'clock, and I had already tidied up my desk and announced to Julie my intention to leave, when the call came from North Carolina.

I ducked back into my office and took it at my desk. "This is Victoria Jones," said the same gone-with-the-wind female voice that had answered when I called. "Mr. Slavin asked me to call you."

"Victoria of Slavin, Jones?"

"No. That would be Gregory Jones. He's dead. No relation. Around here Jones is a pretty common name."

"It's not that rare around here, actually. What did you find out?"

"Nate Greenberg's client has agreed to talk with you."

"You can't just tell me the nature of his business in Boston?"

"No. That's up to his client."

"Give me his number, then."

"I can't. In the first place, it's a she. Second, she doesn't have a phone. Third, she's nervous. Willing, but nervous."

"What are you saying?"

"Piedmont Airlines," she said. "Unless you'd enjoy twenty-four straight hours on a Greyhound."

"If I decide to go down there, will you help me set it up?"

"Mr. Slavin said I should do whatever I could to help you."

"I'll be in touch, then."

I went back to the outer office. Julie had shrouded her computer with its dust cover. She was brushing her hair.

"What're you doing?" I said.

"Getting ready to go."

"One thing?"

She sighed. "I figured."

"See if you can get me a flight to Asheville."

"Asheville, what?"

"North Carolina. Try Piedmont."

She rolled her eyes. "Like for when?"

"Friday. Returning Saturday."

She pressed the tips of her fingers together under her chin and bowed. I went back into my office and poured myself a shot of Jack Daniel's. Flying to Asheville was the sort of move that, if I weighed its merits, I would not make. I recalled the advice of Machiavelli: "It is better to be impetuous than cautious, for fortune is a woman, and if you wish to master her, you must conquer her by force."

Julie—and my ex-wife, Gloria, as well—never hesitated to remind me, whenever I cited these immortal words, that while Machiavelli undoubtedly had been a male chauvinist of the first rank, he might be excused on the grounds of pervasive cultural bias. But a contemporary man who chose voluntarily to quote him deserved gelding, twentieth-century Boston differing as it did from fifteenth-century Florence.

They never let me finish the quote before they started screaming. It went like this: ". . . and it can be seen that she lets herself be overcome by the bold rather than by those who proceed coldly. And therefore, like a woman, she is always a friend to the young, because they are less cautious, fiercer, and master her with greater audacity."

It was odd that, before my consciousness was raised, millimeter by millimeter, kicking and screaming, by the women around me, I found nothing offensive in Machiavelli's metaphor.

I sipped my Tennessee whiskey and stared out at the gloomy skyline. Sulky, sodden clouds had been dribbling misty rain all day. I wondered if Kat would try to beg off our surfcasting expedition. I decided not to let her. If she wanted to fish like a man, she should enjoy misery the way a man does. Anyway, the weather, if anything, would enhance her chance of nailing a bluefish in the surf.

Julie scratched on the door. "Enter."

She came in, bearing a notepad.

"Sit," I said. "Please sit," I hastily amended. "Shot of Black Jack?"

"Sure."

I went to the sideboard and poured a generous finger into a glass. I set it in front of Julie and resumed my seat. She took a quick, nervous sip, then put it down and picked up her notebook. "Departing Logan at 7:05 Friday morning. Forty-minute layover in Charlotte, arriving in Asheville at 10:23 if you don't fly into the side of a mountain, which might serve you right. Returning Saturday. All for a mere $462.50. With seven days advance booking, it's only $170.50. Except you couldn't fly on a Friday, and you'd have to stay over a Saturday. Nobody except Piedmont flies into Asheville from Boston." She put the notebook down and took another sip.

"What's this all about?"

"I did what you asked."

"I mean about me crashing into a mountain."

"How long you known the Scarlett O'Hara broad?"

"You mean Miz Jones." An insight—some connection between Julie's knee-jerk distress when I quoted Machiavelli and her instinctive jealousy whenever I talked to any woman other than my ex-wife—flitted in my mind. There was an irony there. I didn't bother pursuing it. "This is business," I said. "The Winter case."

She smiled. "A case, now, is it?"

I shrugged. "Whatever you'd like to call it. It's Marc's wife, and he's sort of a suspect, and the police are incompetent."

She nodded with mock sagacity. "Ah. You're going to solve it, then."

I lit a Winston. "Maybe."

She stared at me until she made me smile.

"Hey," I said. "It'll be a little adventure. I've never been to Asheville."

"Me neither. I don't feel especially deprived. I've never been to Nome, either."

"I'd like to go to Nome someday," I said.

Julie downed her drink. "The tickets will be waiting for you at the window. You should get there at least a half-hour early."

"Thank you."

"You'll be in tomorrow?"

"Of course. I work here."

"I was wondering," she said.

I called Slavin, Jones. Victoria Jones was unavailable, so I left a message. I would be arriving at 10:23 Friday morning and would call her from the airport.

Julie and I walked out of the office together. "You're leaving early," she observed while we waited for the elevator. "Got a hot date?"

"Going fishing."

"Oh," she said, smiling. She sounded relieved, and I felt an unaccountable pang of guilt.

Actually, I had a date to go fishing. I remembered the way Kat Winter had kissed me in the parking lot. A hot date to go fishing, maybe.

10

KAT WAS WAITING on the side lawn when I
pulled into Des's driveway. She was wearing cutoff jeans,
sneakers, and a pink and white tank top under a man-
sized beige windbreaker. She had found one of Des's old
long-billed fishing caps, which had been liberally stained
with motor oil and fish gore. Her short hair was tucked
up into it.

"I love your chapeau," I said as I climbed out of my
car.

"Daddy says it's good luck."

I squinted up at the sky. "Might rain some more."

She shrugged. "So we get wet."

A pair of surfcasting spinning rods leaned against her
Saab. A big rusted tackle box sat on the driveway. Kat
gestured to the gear. "He said this is all we'd need. You
want to bring some beer?"

"Nope. Don't like to drink and fish. Afterwards we
can stop somewhere if we've got something to cele-
brate."

I cranked the window on the passenger side of my

BMW and pushed the rods in. "Going to be tight quarters for you in the front seat," I said to her.

"I'll just have to squish over close to you."

"It's a short drive."

She climbed in the driver's side and clambered over the console into the other seat. I got in and started up the engine, and had just shifted into reverse when Barney came waddling importantly out from the back of the house. Des was right behind him. He held up his hand. I waited for him to approach my car.

"I just got a call from Marc," he said.

"And?"

"He's at the police station."

"Are they going to arrest him?"

"He didn't know. Fourier wanted to talk to him again."

I glanced sideways at Kat. "Did he want me there?"

Des shook his head. "No. He was just telling me not to wait dinner for him. No, you two go ahead, have a good time. Bring me back a blue. I want to try this recipe. You slather them with mayonnaise and sprinkle on a lot of dill before you grill them."

"Why don't you come along?"

He sighed. "Can't surfcast any more. Damn arthritis."

"We'll get out on the boat sometime."

He forced a smile. "I'd like that."

"Look," I said. "Call Zerk. I think it's time Marc had a lawyer with him."

Des frowned. "You think?"

I nodded. "It'll do no harm."

He waved us away. "I will. Now you two go fishing."

I backed out and headed for Plum Island.

"Why're they hassling Marc again?" said Kat as we drove down High Street. "I thought you said he was in the clear."

I shrugged. "He's about all they've got, maybe. Unless they've come up with new evidence."

"What about the guy who was with Maggie?" Kat's knee was pressing against my thigh. It was hard to ignore.

"I don't know anything about him."

"Do you really think he needs Mr. Garrett with him?"

"Zerk Garrett is the best criminal lawyer I know. He can prevent things from happening. He's better at that sort of thing than I am."

She nodded. I turned left heading for Plum Island.

"Daddy can surfcast fine," said Kat after a few moments. "I think he's just lost his heart for it."

"I'll try to persuade him to take me out on the boat."

Ten minutes later we crossed the causeway and turned right onto the road that bisected the long, narrow island. We parked among a couple dozen other vehicles, the majority of them four-wheel-drive Jeeps and Broncos equipped with rod holders. Beside them, my BMW looked like a poodle on a fox hunt. We unloaded our gear and followed the designated pathway to the outer beach.

The fishermen had strung themselves along the sand at approximately fifty-yard intervals. Some of them were casting from the beach. Others wore chest-high waders and stood out in the crashing surf, presumably closer to where the fish might be lurking. Kat and I took off our sneakers and walked on the cold, hard-packed sand where the sea lapped the beach. We paused at each fisherman to ask what luck. None had taken a bluefish. Nobody seemed the least bit gloomy about it. Picnic baskets, coolers, and unlit lanterns sat in clusters on the beach. These men were here for the night. They had barely started.

We found space to cast several hundred yards down the beach. I snapped dark-bodied Rapalas onto the swivels at the ends of our lines and handed one of the rods to Kat. "Come on," I said. "Might as well get wet. We can wade into the water a little. Then we cast as far as we can."

She took off her windbreaker and followed me into the surf.

The sky was mother-of-pearl, glowing faintly in the dying daylight. The tide was still curling in. It smacked softly against the tilt of the hard sand, oozed forward, then hissed back. The coarse sand jangled like a pocketful of birdshot under the eternal grinding of the sea. Out beyond the surfline the sea was an angry gray-green. It seemed to pitch and roll—the leftover effect of the day's storm. I scanned the water for a swooping swarm of gulls that might signify a school of blues chasing baitfish, but saw none.

Kat and I sloshed in up to our knees. I turned to her. "Okay," I said. "You hold the rod like this." I demonstrated, with my left hand down near the butt end and my right just above the big spinning reel. "Back up the reel just a little and catch the line on your forefinger. Like this." She watched, frowning in concentration, and then imitated me.

"Okay, good," I continued. "Now cock back the bail —that's this piece of wire here—like this." She did. "Now stand back and watch."

I brought the rod over my right shoulder until it was horizontal, bent my knees and arched my back, and heaved mightily. The Rapala sailed out majestically until it was a speck descending from the darkening sky into the ocean.

"Wow," breathed Kat. "That was a good one."

"Average." I was, in truth, very pleased with my manly demonstration, and Kat, bless her, fed my ego.

"Okay," I said. "Now you tuck the butt of the rod into your stomach, or your crotch, or under your arm if you're squeamish about that sort of thing, and you start cranking. Reel as fast as you can, and every couple turns give the rod a yank. Makes the fish think your lure is a frightened baitfish."

Kat frowned at her reel. "Like this?"

I moved closer to her and adjusted her hands into the proper position. "This way," I said. My arm rubbed against her bare shoulder. I stepped back. "Try it."

On her first attempt the line slipped off her finger and the Rapala splatted onto the beach behind her. "Shit," she muttered. I laughed. "What's so funny, Coyne?" she said.

"You in that hat."

She reeled in and repeated the process. This time the plug slapped into the water almost at her feet. She turned to face me. "Don't say a God damn thing."

I held my hands up in surrender. "I didn't say a word."

"Yeah, well I know what you're thinking. It's a man's sport. Right? Huh? Huh?"

I shook my head emphatically. "No. That's not what I was thinking at all."

She smiled. "Good."

"What I was thinking," I said, "was that it's a sport for coordinated people. That's all."

She stuck out her tongue. "Up yours," she said.

"Which," I observed, "may not make you a man, but it sure as hell shows you ain't a lady."

"I thought you'd never notice."

The next time she got it right. It didn't go far, but she did cast the plug in a satisfying arc out into the ocean.

"Not bad. More oomph next time."

"That," she said, "was a hell of a cast."

"For a lady, it would've been."

After a few more tries she seemed to get the hang of it. She became completely engrossed in the mechanics, frowning, biting her lip, and muttering to herself. I moved down the beach from her and began to cast.

I found a pleasant, hypnotic rhythm in it, the sudden uncoiling energy of the cast and the long leisurely reeling in, accompanied in counterpoint by the muffled crash of waves and the gentler lapping of water against the fronts of my thighs. I did not regret the fact that no bluefish struck. Somehow it would have destroyed the harmony.

After perhaps half an hour of it I waded out and sat on the beach. I jammed the butt of my rod into the sand and lit a cigarette. The sun had set behind us. The fishermen down the beach were black smudges on the light water. The sea seemed to have captured the daylight. It radiated a faint greenish fluorescence.

Kat was in up to her hips. Des's silly fishing cap sat cockeyed on her head. She seemed to be casting easily now. Her little cotton singlet was wet from the splash of the surf, and it clung to her body. I admired her grace, the pivot of her torso, the stretch and contraction of the smooth muscles of her arms and shoulders.

As I smoked and watched Kat, I noticed that a cluster of gulls had materialized out beyond where her casts were landing. The birds were darting and diving at the water. I could hear their squawks and cries. They seemed to be moving directly toward Kat.

I yelled at her, and she turned and cupped her ear. I pointed at the gulls. "Out there," I shouted. "Baitfish. The blues're chasing them."

She nodded and cast toward the birds. On her second attempt her rod suddenly arched forward. "Hey! I got one!" she shouted.

I jogged toward her. "Keep your rod up and keep reeling," I said when I was beside her.

"I'm reeling in but the line is going out," she said.

"That's all right. It's the way the drag of the reel is set.

So your line won't break. It'll tire your fish out, pulling against that."

"If it doesn't tire me out first. Boy!"

She gained line slowly. The blue was strong. When it found it couldn't swim straight out to sea, it dashed off parallel with the beach. Kat turned it. Suddenly she said, "It's gone."

"Reel in," I said.

"Damn. It's gone."

Suddenly her rod bucked. "No it's not," she said.

"He was swimming toward you. He's tired now. Back up. You can beach him."

"He's a big one, huh?" she said as the exhausted fish came lolling in on its side.

"A beauty. Five or six pounds. Let me unhook him for you."

"No way, buster. Unhooking them is part of it, right?"

I shrugged. "Be careful. They've got cruel teeth."

She knelt beside the fish and gingerly grabbed the plug where it was hooked onto the side of the fish's mouth. The bluefish thrashed and flopped. Suddenly she said, "Ouch! Dammit!"

The fish fell to the sand, flipped into the water, and after a moment of frenzied churning darted away. "Too bad," I said. "Would've made a nice breakfast for Des."

"Brady . . ."

I looked at her. Her face was contorted under Des's ridiculous cap. She extended her left hand toward me. The Rapala dangled from it like an ornament from a Christmas tree. Two hooks of the rear set of trebles were imbedded in the meaty part at the base of her thumb. I took her hand and examined it. "Both points are in over the barb. How bad does it hurt?"

"Not bad," she said between clenched teeth. Pain glittered in her eyes.

"It'll hurt more when I take them out."

I went to the tackle box and found the one absolutely essential item of fishing gear for the surfcaster, a sturdy pair of long-nosed pliers with built-in wire cutters. I went back and kneeled beside Kat. She clenched her bottom lip tightly between her teeth.

"First," I said, "we get rid of the plug. Hold on."

I cut the treble where it joined the Rapala. Now just the treble hook was left, two of the three hookpoints jammed deep into her hand. "Now comes the hard part." I looked up into her eyes.

"Go ahead," she said.

"I can't back the hooks out. The barbs won't allow it. I'm going to have to work the hooks forward all the way through so that they come out past the barbs. This will hurt. It would hurt anybody, so it's okay to holler and curse if you feel like it. But I've got to snip off those barbs if we're going to get the hooks out. Ready?"

Her narrowed eyes met mine evenly. "Hurt me," she whispered. "Just try it."

I nodded. I held the hook firmly and pushed, twisting it so that the pointed ends would reemerge from her flesh. There was no way to be gentle about it, so I didn't try. The twin points broke her skin. A pair of droplets of blood appeared.

"That was the hard part," I muttered. I continued pushing until the barbs broke through. "Now hold steady so I can snip off those barbs."

She gripped her left wrist in her right hand. She did not quiver or flinch. I placed the pliers flat against her hand and snapped off first one barb and then the other. I looked up at her. "Okay?"

She nodded firmly. "Okay."

I worked the debarbed hooks back out of her hand the way they had gone in. When they were out, she said, "Thank you."

"Had your shots?"

"Yes."

"Suck on it," I told her. "Try to make it bleed. When we get back you should soak it in hot salty water."

She thrust the side of her hand into her mouth. Her eyes were large and gray as they watched me. She mumbled something.

"I couldn't understand you," I said.

We had been kneeling on the wet sand. She hitched herself closer to me. "You suck on it," she said.

She held her hand toward me. I arched my eyebrows. She nodded. "Please," she said softly.

I took her hand in both of mine, as if it were a turkey drumstick, and examined it. The meat at the base of her thumb had begun to swell and darken. There were two sets of punctures, red but bloodless. I glanced up at her. She was staring intently at me. I raised her hand to my mouth and sucked on her wound. She tilted back her head, closed her eyes, and moaned.

I took her hand away from my mouth. "I'm sorry," I said. "That must hurt."

"Oh, Jesus, no," she whispered. "Don't stop. Please."

"Kat . . . ?"

I let go of her hand and stood. She gazed up at me from beneath the bill of Des's fishing cap. I held my hands to her. She lifted her unwounded hand and allowed me to help her stand. She leaned against the front of me. Her cap fell onto the sand. Her hair was in my face. It smelled of the sea.

I held her for a moment, then leaned back and tucked the crook of my forefinger under her chin.

"What was that all about?" I said.

She pushed up on tiptoes and kissed my neck softly. "You jerk," she said.

By the time we got back to where my car was parked it had grown dark. I examined Kat's hand by the dome light. The flesh at the base of her thumb had turned the color of a ripe plum. "I think I should take you to the hospital," I said.

"Just take me home."

I shrugged. "Okay."

Kat's condo was on the second floor of a square old converted warehouse, in the rear, overlooking the river. She had decorated it in white and black. Starkly geometric furniture. Vast expanses of bare wood and glass and chrome. An enormous abstract painting dominated one wall, a rendering, as well as I could interpret, of a yellow triangular sail spattered by arterial bleeding. Strangely, the colors worked perfectly in Kat's room.

She disappeared into the bathroom. I found a big bowl and filled it with scalding water from the tap. I poured in some salt and set the bowl on the dining table.

She came out barefoot wrapped in a terrycloth robe that stopped halfway down her thighs. She had brushed out her hair and done something to her eyes that made them look larger.

"Sit," I said. "Stick your hand in there."

She sat. "Want a drink?" she said.

"Beer in the fridge?"

"Yes. One for me, too."

There was a six-pack of Budweiser on the bottom shelf. Her brand surprised me. I'd have expected something imported, expensive, and low-caloried. I took two cans, cracked them both, and placed one beside her where she sat, her wounded hand poised over the steaming bowl of water.

"I can't. It's too hot."

"The hotter you can stand it the better."

She grabbed the wrist of her injured left hand with her right and forced it into the bowl. She winced. I saw her mouth move. She was counting. ". . . ten!" she said, and removed her hand. After a moment, she repeated the process, getting up to fifteen. She was, I decided, a strong and willful woman.

We sipped our beer and I smoked while Kat soaked her hand. When the bowl of water had cooled down, I brought her a towel. She dried her hand and then held it toward me. I took it and she stood. "Come on," she said.

She led me into the living-room area. She pushed me gently onto the sofa. Then she turned on her stereo. She found a station that was playing Charlie Byrd. She turned to me with arched eyebrows. I nodded.

She came and sat beside me. She tucked her bare legs under her and lay her cheek against my shoulder. "Thank you for tonight," she said softly. "It was a huge kick, catching that fish."

"He caught you, actually."

She turned over her swollen hand in her lap. "I won't be able to play the violin for a few days. It'll be fine."

She hitched herself closer to me. I pried off my shoes. I lay my head against the back of the sofa, put my arm around Kat's shoulders, and closed my eyes.

"Brady?"

"Mmm?"

"What's going to happen to my brother?"

"He didn't do it," I said. "Andy Pavelich can vouch for him. Zerk'll take good care of him."

She was silent for a minute. "That's good," she said. "I think one more thing would kill my father."

"Des is tougher than you think."

"He isn't tough at all," she said quietly. "He has never recovered from . . ." She stopped.

"I've always wondered," I said.

"What?"

"When you and your mother—when you went away . . ."

I let the question trail away. Kat didn't answer.

I felt her weight shift. Then her lips were on my

cheek. She kissed me softly. I could feel her breast press against my arm. Her hand crept onto my chest, then to the back of my head. Her mouth opened on mine. A tiny moan came from the back of her throat. My hand touched the smooth skin on her bare leg and slid under the hem of her robe to her hip. She wore no underwear. Her mouth twisted and pressed against mine. I touched her robe over her breast. Her hand covered mine, pressing, urging.

"Wait," she whispered. "Please." She pushed at my hand.

I moved away from her. She tugged at the short hem of her robe and hugged herself.

"Kat, look," I said.

She touched my lips with her forefinger. She tried to smile, and didn't quite make it. She took a deep breath and squeezed her eyes shut for a moment. She shook her head slowly back and forth and smiled. "I'm sorry," she said.

I shrugged. "It's all right."

"I can't."

"Don't worry about it, Kat."

"You want to finish your beer?"

"I probably should go."

"You don't have to."

I got up and she took my hand and walked me to the door. I opened it and turned. She peered at me, frowning. "Brady?"

"Kat, it's all right."

She reached up and touched my cheek with the palm of her hand. "Thanks," she said. "For everything."

I nodded. "Good night, Kat."

11

"SO THIS COP, this Fourier, he come out," said Zerk, his grin broad in his strong black face, "and he ask can he help me. So I tell him I want to see Marc Winter, he my client. And Fourier, he smile, like maybe he gonna let me, then again, maybe he not. He ask me what I wanna see him for. I repeat to him Marc my client, I got a right to see him, 'specially since they ain't even arrested the man."

Zerk swung his big frame from the corner of my desk, where he had been perched, and settled into the chair. He gave me a big white-toothed grin. He enjoyed his self-parody. Listening to him, it would be hard to tell that he had been magna cum at Tufts and third in his class at law school. He took a sip of coffee and peered at me from over the rim.

"You *are* quite sensitive to racial innuendo," I said mildly.

"Yassah, boss, I shore is. And you isn't."

I shrugged. "I try to distinguish ordinary rudeness from racially motivated rudeness."

He grinned. "Safe to say, you have a different perspective on that sort of thing from me." Xerxes Garrett, whose middle-linebacker construction was not at all disguised by his gray three-piece suit, had clerked for me several years earlier in exchange for the tutoring I gave him for the Law Boards. He had since become a first-rate criminal lawyer, and while much of his practice consisted of *pro bono* work for poor families in Dorchester and Roxbury, he did enjoy defending white people. "I like the way they depend on you. How they call you up for reassurance, and you've got to soothe them like they were children. Anyway," he added, "it pays well. You taught me the importance of that."

When Marc Winter was arrested on the drug charge a few years earlier, it was Zerk who I asked to take the case.

"Finally," he continued, "I say to the cop, Fourier, I say, 'Listen. I wanna know where my client's at.' And Fourier, he tip his head over to the side, like he the teacher and I the dumb burrhead student, the pompous prick, and he say, 'You should never end a sentence with a preposition.' So I nod my head like I just learned something important, and I say, 'Oh, right. Thank you for reminding me. So where's my client at, *asshole*?' "

"Perfect," I said.

Zerk grinned and nodded. "I understand you're taking a real interest in this case," he said.

I shrugged. "There's some interesting aspects of it."

" 'Interesting aspects,' " he repeated. "You do have a nice way with words, boss. You never end your sentences with prepositions. This case might be less complicated than meets the eye, though, actually."

"You think Marc killed Maggie?"

Zerk shook his head. "He might've. Says he didn't. I talked with him a long time last night. Then I talked to his old man, the minister. I try to look at this as if I were prosecuting it. Look at what we got. We got this young wife of dubious background who's out gettin' it on with some other guy in her father-in-law's boat. That certainly takes care of Marc's motive. Opportunity? We've got a witness who sees him drive up and call the cops about the crime without his going to the boat, which clearly means he already knew there was a corpse in there. Nobody can account for the husband's whereabouts between nine and the time the cops show up at the marina."

I lifted up my hand. "Didn't Marc tell you about Andrea Pavelich?"

He nodded. "Yup. He told me. He even told me you talked to her. He told me about your encounter with the lady's old man, too. You're losing a step, boss. But he won't let me talk to her, and he won't ask her to testify for him. Which means, thinking now like a prosecutor, it's no different than if he's got no witness."

"Well, I *did* talk to her, and she *does* verify his story."

"But she's got this mean sombitch husband who beats the shit out of her whenever she looks sideways at another man."

"That she does. I can verify that, too."

Zerk sighed. "If she won't testify, it's like she doesn't exist."

"I think she's telling the truth."

"The truth isn't necessarily the point, bossman," said Zerk. "You taught me that. It's evidence that's the point. Anyways, young Massa Winter wouldn't let me talk to his gal. But he said he'd talk to her, try to persuade her to agree to testify, work out some way to handle her husband." Zerk shook his head back and forth slowly.

"You don't believe she told me the truth, do you?"

He put his elbows on my desk and leaned toward me. "A prosecutor assumes she's lying, that she was there, maybe participated in the murder. A prosecutor figures Marc and Andy, they go to the boat and hear Maggie and her boyfriend groaning and thrashing around. So they wait till the fella leaves, go aboard. Maggie's lying there in the berth, all naked and satiated. Maybe Marc asks her what in hell she thinks she's doing, and she sees Andy there and says she figures she's doing what he wants to do. So Marc and Maggie have an argument. He whacks her a few times. Andy's standing there. When Marc realizes what he's done, he tells Andy she's an accessory, she's in trouble like him, but she can cover for him, they can cover for each other. She's worried about Al, but she's worried worse about herself. So they make up a story they both can stick to. A prosecutor'd love to get that gal on the witness stand." Zerk smiled at me. "That's something else you taught me, boss."

"What's that?"

"To think like a prosecutor."

"Well, hell, I taught you everything you know."

"One thing you taught me that you keep forgetting yourself."

"What's that?"

"You always say the commonest things most commonly happen."

"Meaning in this case?"

"Meaning husbands most commonly beat hard on wayward wives."

"That's how the cops see it."

"It is. Less commonly do we have mysterious attorneys from North Carolina on the scene getting knifed in their motel rooms ten miles away having some convoluted connection to the wife getting whacked." Zerk frowned at me. "I want to know what you're thinking."

I held out my arms, palms up. "This Greenberg called me, then got killed. That interests me. He was seen with Maggie the day before they both got murdered. That seems to me a connection."

Zerk held up his hand. "Whoa. What I understand,

you don't know whether this dead one is the same Greenberg who called you, and you don't know if he's the same bald guy your retarded friend saw with Maggie Winter."

"He was driving the same kind of car. And I don't know any other Nathan Greenberg."

"What if Snooker Lynch was lying?"

"Why should he lie?"

"That," said Zerk, "is the question the prosecutor asks. A good question. Point is, this Mr. Lynch doesn't sound like the most impressive witness. Meantime the cops are assuming the commonest thing most commonly happens."

"They're going after Marc."

He nodded. "Looks that way. Local cops want to see if they can crack the case before the state cops."

"But they haven't arrested Marc."

"Not yet."

"Sounds to me as if Andy Pavelich is a key."

"Marc's going to talk to her. And what're you doing?"

"I'm flying down to North Carolina tomorrow," I said.

"Why?"

I shrugged. "Just curious, maybe. I want to see if this Greenberg is the same one who called me. If so, why. And if there's any connection between him and Maggie."

"Bringing your fishing pole?"

"Rod," I said. "It's called a rod. And no, I'm not."

"Nice trout fishing in North Carolina, they say."

"I've heard that."

Zerk unfolded himself from the chair and stood up. "Anyway, boss, you don't have to worry about Marc Winter any more."

"Why not?"

"Because I'm defending him."

"We will all sleep better."

After Zerk left I put through a call to Doc Adams's office in Concord. Doc is a master oral surgeon and one of my fishing buddies. He spent some time in the western part of North Carolina a few years earlier. I intended to allow him to tell me tall tales of fabulous trout fishing in the mountain streams, which would persuade me to stow some fly-fishing gear on the airplane and maybe stay over in Asheville an extra day. It would be a hedge against the likelihood that my pursuit of the Nathan Greenberg mystery would turn out to be another in a lifetime full of wild goose chases.

I got Doc's answering service. Dr. Adams, a friendly young female with a faint trace of Dublin in her voice told me, was on vacation. She could reach him if it was an emergency. I said it wasn't. She said he'd be in his office on Monday. I told her that was too late. She seemed genuinely disappointed that she couldn't help me. She said he checked in every afternoon, she could give him a message.

"Okay," I said. "Ask him if he heard about the couple who didn't know the difference between Vaseline and putty."

She giggled. "Shall I tell him the answer, too?"

"No. Let him try to figure it out."

"Will you tell me?"

"You've got to promise not to tell Doc."

"I promise."

"Their windows all fell out."

I spent the rest of Thursday dictating memos to Julie and chatting with clients on the telephone. For most of my clients, most of the time, the ability to chat with a lawyer about hypothetical problems is worth a lot of money. For me, being available to chat with wealthy clients about imaginary legal issues is my work, for which I am rewarded with handsome retainers. Sometimes real problems appear. Usually they don't. People—especially very rich people—get nervous when they don't have problems. Not having a problem becomes a problem. My peculiar legal specialty is helping wealthy old people feel comfortable about not having problems.

I rarely am asked to write articles for learned journals about my specialty.

Sometimes my clients actually do get divorced or arrested. Sometimes they decide to buy a new business, or sell an old one. They set up trusts for children and grandchildren. They look for tax dodges. Eventually, they die. All of these activities require planning, consulting, conferring. Options need to be studied. Game plans must be drawn up.

It keeps me busy.

It does not preoccupy me.

My friends marvel at my law practice. How easy it is, how lucrative.

How boring.

They usually seem envious.

I explain to them that I fish for trout. Often and avidly. Fishing, I tell my friends, is a great deal like sex. When it's good, it's absolutely wonderful. And when it's bad, it's still pretty damn good.

In fast-moving parts of eastern rivers, small trout lie in shallow riffles. They feed eagerly. They strike willingly at almost any sort of artificial fly that floats near them. Sometimes, I tell my friends, I will cast to these fish. They pose no particular challenge. I never doubt that I will catch several of them.

Fishing for them keeps me busy.

It does not preoccupy me.

I am also acquainted, I tell my friends, with a large brown trout who lives in a slow moving stretch of the lower Swift River. He lies behind a sunken log up against a steep bank which is overhung by birch trees whose branches nearly brush the surface of the water. My brown trout feeds on the small insects that get trapped in the sluggish eddy, where it is impossible to make a dry fly float in a natural manner. He weighs at least four pounds, and I would like to persuade him to strike at my fly.

I like to sit on the bank and smoke and ponder the problem. What fly might that old brown trout take? How can I cast it without spooking him? Should I wait until evening? Perhaps come at night, or before sunrise in the morning, to fish for him?

So far, I haven't actually cast toward that brown trout. I figure I'm going to get one chance. I want to make sure I've thought it through.

It's a problem of tactics and execution that I have not yet resolved.

This brown trout does preoccupy me.

Occasionally, my law practice brings me the equivalent of that Swift River brown trout, a difficult case, a challenge, a situation unprecedented in my experience that requires me, metaphorically, to negotiate overhanging branches, deceptive, swirling currents, and a shrewd, experienced adversary. The death of Maggie Winter struck me as one of those. Zerk may have been correct. Perhaps it was what it appeared to be, a jealous husband hitting his wayward wife too hard, what the police liked to call a "domestic situation." Sad, tragic, and utterly commonplace.

But I didn't think so.

I disembarked in the Asheville airport, looked around for a pay phone, and heard my name on the public address system. "Brady Coyne from Boston, you're wanted at the information counter."

I lookcd around, saw the sign, and went over, my single flight bag slung over my shoulder. I stepped up to the window when I felt a hand on my arm. I turned. "Mr. Coyne?"

She was about fifty, rail thin and leathery. Her gray-streaked black hair hung long and straight down her back. She wore sandals and jeans and a short-sleeved white blouse. No makeup, no jewelry. She had a long, bumpy nose, heavy-lidded dark eyes, and a broad expressive mouth which was now smiling at me.

"Yes. I'm Coyne."

She held out her hand. "Victoria Jones, at your service."

I shook hands with her. "I didn't expect you to greet me."

"Southern hospitality. I also booked you a room. I hope you don't mind. It's just a motel, but it's clean and convenient. There's a restaurant next door that's decent if you like genuine southern barbecue."

"I love genuine southern barbecue."

"How long are you staying?"

"Returning tomorrow. I just wanted to talk to Greenberg's client."

"Too bad. There's a lot to see in Asheville."

"Another time, maybe."

She steered me out of the airport, chatting about the Biltmore mansion, the minor league baseball team, mountain music, clogging. We got into her car, a Ford Escort, and ten minutes later she deposited me at my motel, an establishment that appeared to be considerably more prosperous than the one in Danvers, Massachusetts, where Nathan Greenberg had gone to die.

"Here's the drill," said Victoria as we sat in the Escort outside the motel office. "Lanie—that's her name, Lanie

Horton—she starts work at four. She waits tables in town, but she lives outside town. She's expecting us at one. So I figured you'd like to clean up, grab a bite. I'll pick you up—let's see, it's about eleven now—say around twelve thirty?"

"That sounds fine," I said. "But you really didn't need to go to all this trouble."

She shrugged her bony shoulders. "Lanie is our client. It's how she wants it. She's a very proper young lady. She wouldn't meet you in a public place. In her home, she wants me there. Anyway, she's a bit nervous about this. She's quite upset about what happened to Nate. Figures somehow it's her fault. So she feels guilty, which I guess is why she agreed to meet you."

"Well," I said, "I really appreciate all you've done."

"No problem," she said.

I checked into my room and changed out of my suit into chino pants and a blue shirt. Then I walked to the restaurant, which featured high-backed booths, dim lights, country music over the speakers, and a luncheon menu similar to those in most Boston restaurants.

My waitress was blond, buxom, and young. She served me a cheeseburger and iced tea for about half what I would have paid in my city.

I went back to the motel and sat on an aluminum chair beside the pool to smoke and wait for Victoria Jones. Three little girls frolicked in the shallow end. Two of them were trying to persuade the third to duck her head all the way under. They were kind, patient, and imaginative about it. Two young women—mothers, I assumed, although they looked young enough to be teen-aged babysitters—watched the little ones closely. I caught fragments of their conversation, not enough to understand the words, but enough to identify their accents. New Jersey.

The little girl bobbed under and blew bubbles. She

came up sputtering and laughing. Her two teachers shouted. The two women by the pool applauded. I joined in the applause.

Victoria showed up on the dot of twelve thirty. I got up and headed for her car. The little swimmers yelled "Bye-bye" to me. I waved and smiled.

As we drove through the city, Asheville seemed to me to be more like a large, well-kept suburb than a city. I saw no skyscrapers. The residential areas seemed to merge seamlessly with the business districts. I mentioned this to Victoria.

"Best city in the U. S. of A.," she told me. "That's not just my opinion. Couple Yankee boys wrote a book a few years ago that says so. Climate, culture, nice people, everything you'd want." She glanced sideways at me. "I came here from Oregon to get away from my husband. That was twenty-seven years ago. Never wanted to go anywhere else. Anyway, there's plenty of work for a lawyer here."

I wasn't aware of leaving the city limits until Victoria told me that we had entered Woodfin, where Lanie Horton lived. We followed a wide river, turned off onto a winding two-lane road that seemed to be climbing into the forest, and pulled to a stop beside a mobile home on the edge of the woods.

A stark white picket fence demarcated a tiny front yard. The grass was freshly mown. A picnic table and benches sat out front. Roses grew on a trellis that leaned against the trailer beside the door. A very old Pinto hatchback, originally yellow but painted in several patches with flat black, hunkered under a carport attached to the end.

I read in this yard poverty and pride.

Victoria and I clambered out of her Escort. As we did, the front door of the trailer opened and a girl came out. She carried a pitcher in one hand and three glasses in the other. She wore red running shorts, sneakers without socks, and a man's white shirt with the tails knotted across her stomach.

She moved coltishly. Her legs were long, knobby at the knees. She had narrow hips, a thin waist, not much bosom. Her black hair was pulled back into a short ponytail tied with a bright red ribbon.

She moved to the picnic table and put down the pitcher and glasses. "Well, come on in, y'all," she said to me and Victoria.

We walked through the gate and sat at the picnic table. Up close, Lanie Horton looked a little older than from a distance. She had tiny squint lines at the corners of her eyes, and a way of setting her mouth that made one believe she had experienced some grown-up problems. She wasn't fourteen, which had been my first guess. Eighteen or nineteen, maybe.

"Iced tea," said Lanie. "Made in the sun."

She lifted her eyebrows at me, and I nodded. "Perfect."

She poured three glasses.

"This is Mr. Coyne from Boston," said Victoria.

"Ah figured that out," said Lanie, grinning nervously.

"I really appreciate your seeing me," I said to her.

She shrugged. "Don't make no difference to me."

"I'm trying to figure out why Mr. Greenberg was in Boston."

"And why he got killed, huh?"

"Yes."

"I know why he was in Boston."

"I understood you did."

"At least, if he was there on account of why I hired him."

"That was the only case that would take him to Boston," said Victoria.

"Not why he was killed, though," said Lanie. "I don't know nothing about that."

I nodded.

"He was trying to find my parents for me," said Lanie.

12

LANIE SIPPED her iced tea, then licked her upper lip. She frowned at me. "See, Mr. Coyne, I'm adopted. I didn't find this out until me 'n' Eddie were planning to get married. I had to get a birth certificate before we could get a marriage license. I figured out from the birth certificate that I was adopted. My momma never told me. She brought me up as if I was her own kid. I think she really plain forgot she adopted me. She loved me so much. I was her only child. I think she just fooled herself into thinking I was her real baby. When I saw that on my birth certificate, at first I was mad at her. What kind of right did she have to pretend I was her natural child? I was going to tell her what I knew. Make her explain herself. Who did she think she was, keeping something like that from me? But then I thought about it. What difference did it really make? She loved me, she always took good care of me. What right did I have to spoil it for her?"

She appealed to me with raised eyebrows. I noticed how dark her eyes were. I nodded.

"None," she said. "I had no right. So I never said

anything to her. Still haven't. I think it would've really hurt her. It would've killed her if she knew I knew, and if she thought for a minute that I didn't love her like a real momma. And the thing is, I do love her. She's been real good to me. A real momma, in every way. So if it wasn't for what happened, I suppose I would've just forgotten about it. Because once I thought it all the way through, I knew I wasn't hung up on it, and I knew I shouldn't let on to her. But now, after what happened, I really do have to find out about my real parents." She paused to sip.

"You didn't mention your father," I said.

She shrugged. "He ran out on Momma when I was little. It used to bother me. Funny. Soon as I found out I was adopted, and he wasn't my real daddy, it stopped bothering me. That was one good thing about it, I guess. Getting over that feeling about my daddy. Anyways, so Eddie and me got married and I got pregnant, which was how we wanted it. Lotta folks figured it happened the other way around, but it didn't. Eddie's got a good job drivin' trucks, and he's gone a lot. It gets lonely. But he's real good to me, and when I wanted to wait until we were married proper, that was okay with him." She hesitated and looked away from me. "The rest is kinda hard to talk about."

Victoria reached across the picnic table and touched her arm. Lanie smiled wanly at her and put her hand on top of Victoria's. "It's okay," she said. She looked up at me. "See, I lost my baby. That was in April. He was—I'd been carrying him for five months. A little boy. Couple weeks later the doctor's office called me, wanted me to go in and meet with the doctor. Eddie was on the road, so I went in by myself. The doctor started asking me a lot of questions about me and Eddie. What we've been sick from. Did we ever have—you know, venereal disease. He got real personal, especially asking about Eddie. Did he shack up on the road? Made me almost mad, except the doctor was so professional and all, like it didn't matter to him. And he wanted to know all about my momma and daddy, and Eddie's too. And going back to grandparents even."

I thought I saw what had happened. "A complete medical history of both you and your husband, then?"

Lanie nodded. "Right. And I told him everything I knew. But finally I said to him, I said, 'Why are you asking me all this?' And he told me. That—that my baby, my little boy, he died—he miscarried—because he had some problem that was either my fault or Eddie's."

"A genetic defect," I said.

She nodded. "Something that might mean—"

She stopped and bent to her iced tea. When she looked up at me her eyes were shining. "Might mean I shouldn't have any more babies," she finished. "That they'd all be—they wouldn't be able to live, or they'd be retarded or something." She tried to smile. "Anyway, I felt stupid, answering all those questions about Momma and my daddy. Because they had nothing to do with my baby's genes. I was adopted. So I told the doctor that. He said it was real important that I try to find out about my biological parents, see if I could get them to talk to him. I told him I didn't know how to do that. He said I should try a lawyer."

"So you came to us," said Victoria.

Lanie shook her head. "Not at first. I didn't know what to do. Eddie's working so hard so we can get a down payment on a house, and I put everything I make from waitressing into it, too. At first I decided just to go ahead and have another baby, take my chances. But then I realized it would about break Eddie's heart to go through that again. Mine, too. So I went back to the doctor and told him what my problem was. He said he'd see what he could do. Couple days later Mr. Greenberg came to the restaurant. He told me he was a lawyer, he was going to help me. I said that was nice but I couldn't afford a lawyer. He said there was some sort of special fund for things like that. I wouldn't have to pay him." She peered at Victoria. "This didn't sound right to me, to tell you the truth. And I hate to say anything bad about somebody who's—who's dead—but . . ."

Victoria smiled. "Nate was not a particularly pleasant man," she said to me.

Lanie nodded. "It wasn't like he said anything or did anything you could put your finger on."

"He was a sleazy man," said Victoria. "He oozed sleaze. He couldn't help it."

"Anyhow," continued Lanie, "I told him no. I wouldn't hear of anybody doing something for me without getting paid. He argued, but I can be stubborn when I want to be. Finally he went away. The next day the doctor called me at work. Bawled me out. Tried to explain that Mr. Greenberg was going to get paid, that he was good at doing that kind of work, and that it was important. The doctor is real nice. So I said okay, and Mr. Greenberg came back the next day. He asked me some questions."

"Like what?" I said.

She frowned. "Like where I was born—where it said on my birth certificate, I mean. Some stuff about my momma. I told him I didn't want him to talk to her, and he agreed to that. Said it probably wasn't necessary. So that was like a couple weeks ago."

"How old are you, Lanie?" I said.

"Eighteen. Going on nineteen."

"And where *were* you born, according to your birth certificate?"

"Winston-Salem."

"And as far as you know, Nathan Greenberg was in Boston looking for one or both of your parents?"

She shrugged. "If he was there on my account, that's why."

"Did you talk to him again?"

She shook her head. "No." She sighed and slumped her shoulders. "And I never will. So I'm right back where I started from."

"Don't worry," said Victoria. "Somebody else will take your case."

"For nothing?"

She nodded. "Don't worry."

On the ride back to Asheville, Victoria explained the policy of Slavin, Jones on *pro bono* work. "Twenty percent of the company time must be billed to *pro bono*. It works out evenly for all of us over the long haul. Nate Greenberg did less than his share, actually, so Mr. Slavin thought this would be a good one for him. We handle an awful lot of custody and abuse stuff as well as all sorts of small criminal things. These are mountain folks out here. Good, smart people, but they aren't that sophisticated in the law. They forget to pay their taxes, ignore summonses and subpoenas, smack around their kids and wives, and end up getting arrested and hauled to one court or another. Or we get referrals. Like Lanie's doctor calling us." She glanced sideways at me and grinned. She had a wide, expressive mouth, and her smile took ten years off her looks. "I don't know why I should lecture you on what attorneys do."

"I have a different sort of clientele," I said, "but I've done *pro bono* now and then. More or less by accident."

"Anyway," she said, "I suppose we'll get someone else on Lanie's case, now that Nate's off it. Probably me."

"Well," I said, "If you're ever in Boston . . ."

I thought about it that evening while I had barbecue at Hawgie's, the little restaurant next door to my motel in Asheville. Shredded smoked pork, hot tangy sauce, with hush puppies and barbecued beans, washed down with beer.

I thought about it Saturday afternoon while my Piedmont jet circled over Logan International Airport in Boston awaiting landing instructions.

I thought about it while I watched the Red Sox beat Chicago on the black-and-white television set in my apartment Saturday night.

I thought about it before I went to sleep that night, and when I awoke the next morning, and in my car as I drove to Belchertown, Massachusetts, Sunday afternoon.

I thought about it while I sat on the bank of the Swift River and watched my own personal two-foot brown trout fin in the shade of a partially submerged treetrunk and tried to calculate how I might fool him into trying to eat an artificial fly.

Every time I thought about it, it came out the same way.

Maggie Winter was Lanie Horton's mother.

I got to the office early Monday morning. The first thing I did was load up the Mr. Coffee machine and switch it on.

The second thing I did was call Zerk Garrett.

He was still home. I knew he would be. The curse of insomnia hadn't hit him yet. I kept telling him to wait until he turned forty.

"Yo," he said cheerfully into the phone.

"Yo, yo self," I said.

"Hiya, bossman."

"I got some news for you."

"Me too," he said.

"Me first. I figured out what happened. Ready?"

"Shoot."

So I told him about my trip to Asheville, about Lanie Horton's search for her biological parents, about Nate Greenberg's mission to Boston, about Maggie, and about how I figured either Maggie killed Greenberg, or Greenberg killed Maggie. Then I said, "What do you think so far?"

"Real interesting," said Zerk. "But so far, I don't see how all this helps my client."

"I guess it doesn't," I admitted. "Since Greenberg and Maggie couldn't have killed each other, it does seem to leave Marc as a logical suspect for one kill or the other. Of course, if Andy Pavelich is telling the truth, Marc's off the hook anyway. You had a chance to talk to her yet?"

"I said I had news for you," said Zerk.

"Okay. Let's have it."

"Andy Pavelich got shot to death Saturday night."

I took a deep breath. "Oh, Jesus, Zerk."

"Yeah. Young kid. Little babies at home."

"Who? Not—?"

"No, not Marc. Marc's covered on this one. They're holding the girl's husband."

"Big Al," I said. "Mean-tempered son of a bitch. Figures. Did he beat her up?"

"Nope. Shot her in the chest and the throat."

"They got the goods on Al, huh?"

"He called the cops himself, is how I hear it. They showed up, he was stomping around the house, drunker'n a hootie owl. That's all I hear."

I was silent for a minute. Then I said, "Oh, my God, Zerk."

"What, boss?"

"If Al killed Andy . . ."

"What?"

"If he killed her, it could be—see, I talked with her. With Andy. At the restaurant, where she works. About the night Maggie got killed. And Al came by and saw me talking to her. And he jumped me in the parking lot. Marc dragged him off me. He threatened me. And—and he threatened Andy. See what I mean?"

"You think this guy murdered his wife because he saw you talking to her?"

"Maybe. Or maybe after he saw us talking he got her to admit she had been fooling around with Marc Winter. Either way, it's my fault, Zerk."

"Now, listen, you dumb shit," he said. "Listen good. Either way, it's Al's fault, not yours. Hear me? Al, or whoever killed the lady, it's their fault, not yours. And don't give me any of your for whom the bell tolls horseshit, either."

"You're right," I sighed.

"Course I'm right."

"It doesn't change how I feel."

"You'll get over it."

"Maybe," I said doubtfully. "They got the goods on Al, then?"

"I don't know. I didn't inquire. All I know is that Marc's alibi is down the tubes. Not to be insensitively objective about the whole thing."

"Assuming she was telling the truth."

"Yeah," he said, "and not lying for him."

"Or involved herself."

"Or that."

"The way I see it," I said after a minute, "is we have three murders. Maggie, Greenberg, and now Andy Pavelich. And we've got three different murder weapons. Blunt instrument, serrated kitchen knife, gun. Three different motives, probably. And it looks like three different murderers."

"One of which might be my client," he said.

"Yeah. Unless we're missing something."

"We are missing something," said Zerk.

"Yeah? What's that?"

"The hole in your scenario."

"What hole?"

"Hey. Don't get touchy. The problem with all this is Maggie. One way or the other, she's at the center of all this. And nobody seems to know much about her. Not even her husband. Okay, so she got knocked up when she was a kid, and this Lanie Horton is her daughter, and Greenberg tracked her down, and maybe one of them killed the other one. But maybe—"

"Maybe none of those things is true," I finished. "Is that it?"

"I'd just like it better if I knew more about her." Zerk paused. "Wouldn't you?"

"I suppose," I said.

"Don't sulk."

"I wasn't sulking. I was thinking."

"Oh-oh," said Zerk.

13

THE PARKING LOT at the Night Owl was packed on that midsummer Monday evening—predominantly pickup trucks and four-wheel-drive wagons bearing almost as many license plates from Maine and New Hampshire as from Massachusetts, but a respectable smattering of Ford wagons, Toyotas, and here and there a Mercedes and a Porsche.

Strippers do have a democratic appeal.

Inside, smoky haze hung thick from the low ceiling. A rectangular stage jutted into the middle of the big brightly lit room. On three sides of the stage, randomly placed tables and chairs crowded close. Those nearest the stage were jammed with people. All men. Above the stage, a glass ball rotated slowly, breaking the lights into a million multicolored pieces and swirling them around the room. A low wrought-iron railing ran around the three sides of the stage—a symbolic separation of the audience from the performers. The loud insistent beat of rock music buzzed and whined through an overstimulated amplification system, distorting the words that were being sung beyond any possible comprehension, had anybody cared, which did not seem likely.

The girl on the stage was mouthing them, however. It was startling to walk from a soft, starry summer night into a room where a beautiful young girl clad only in a thin gold ankle bracelet gyrated mindlessly, her eyes closed, her face blank, with maybe a hundred men gathered close to the stage, staring up at her.

An L-shaped bar stood to the right of the stage. Two girls in jeans and T-shirts sat side by side at one end, ignoring the performance. Otherwise, all the patrons of the Night Owl were clustered near the stage. I went over to the bar and perched on a stool. I assumed this was the same bar where a black-haired stripper named Maggie had scared away two bikers with a hatpin, so impressing Marc Winter that he married her.

I cocked an elbow on the bar and half-pivoted my body so that I could watch the show. The song ended. The girl on stage flashed a quick insincere smile, made a short bow, and ducked behind the curtain. A moment later another tune, using the term loosely, exploded from the speakers. The girl came back. She began to parade slowly in front of the guys who were leaning their forearms on the wrought-iron railing. Every few feet she stopped, spread her legs wide, and bent her body backwards until her long blond hair touched the floor behind her. She certainly was limber. The boys in the front rows got an eyeful and showed their appreciation by whistling and clapping. The audience response was similar to the one Larry Bird got whenever he canned a three-pointer from the corner.

"Beer?"

I turned. The bartender was large and black-bearded and squinty-eyed. He sported a short ponytail in back. He wore a black T-shirt. On it an owl winked lasciviously.

"What've you got in bottles?"

"Bud."

"That's it?"

"That's what's cold. Want one?"

"Sure."

He plunked it in front of me a moment later. No glass, not that I would have used one anyway. "Two fifty."

I fished out a five and gave it to him. He put the change on the bar in front of me. I left it there. I rotated to watch the dancer. She was doing a new trick. She turned her back to a pod of guys in shirtsleeves and loosened neckties who might've driven over from one of the high-tech outfits in southern New Hampshire. Stiff-legged, she shuffled backwards toward them until her heels touched the railing. Then she bent forward at the waist so that she could look at the computer guys upside-down through her legs. I saw her reach between her legs toward the railing, pause to say something to one of her admirers, wiggle her ass a couple times, then stand up. She repeated this odd dance several times before the song ran out.

I turned to the bartender, who had his chin propped in his hands, his elbows on the bar near me. "What's she doing?"

"Selling them a peek."

"I don't get it."

"They put dollar bills on top of the railing. She's retrieving them. Gives them a good look at her snatch." He shrugged. "You ask me, you seen one you seen 'em all."

"You worked here long?"

"Couple months is all. Not that much work for a thirty-five-year-old guy who keeps changing his mind about what he's going to write his doctoral thesis about. So I've been bouncing from one job to another. This one here pays pretty well, considering about all I have to do is open beer bottles and put them on the waitresses' trays."

"What's your area?"

" 'Scuse me?"

"Your thesis. What is your academic specialty?"

"The transcendentalists." He laughed. "Emerson would've loved a place like this. Imagine Thoreau coming into the Night Owl."

The music throbbed to a stop, the stripper waved at her fans, and a harsh woman's voice rasped over the speakers. "Dusty Knight, ladies and gentlemen. Ain't she a beautiful girl? What a dancer! What a great body! Let's give Dusty Knight a big round of applause."

The boys by the stage responded enthusiastically.

"Don't forget," continued the woman's three-pack-a-day amplified voice, "Tuesday is amateur night at the Night Owl. So you fellas bring your gals on down here so you can show 'em off. Who knows? Maybe one of 'em'll be a star, get herself a job here at the Night Owl. And Thursday is ladies night at the Night Owl. Tell your girlfriends and wives and tell your grandmothers. We've got a batch of hunky men on our Night Owl stage every Thursday. Straight from *Playgirl*. Out of the class of all you horny little wienies. Heh-heh-heh."

"Who's the one with the voice?" I asked the bartender.

"That's Ray."

"Ray? She is a woman, isn't she?"

He laughed, a crude imitation of Ray's wickedly suggestive heh-heh-heh. "She's a woman, all right. She's no lady, but she's a woman. Owns this joint. Raybelle's my boss."

"How do I get to talk to her?"

"Unzip your fly. She'll find you."

"No, really."

Raybelle's voice was introducing the next performer,

a "sweet southern siren" named Sally Flame, who turned out to be a redhead. She pranced onto the stage wearing a skintight sequined gown and stiletto heels. She made one mincing trip up the stage, one back, and then flicked a few snaps and the gown peeled off, revealing a black lace bra and G-string and a great deal of Sally Flame. She marched around the stage in this getup for a while, her movements completely uncoordinated with the music, offering no pretense at dancing. She chatted and exchanged wisecracks with her audience.

"What do you want to talk to Raybelle about?" said the bartender.

"Someone who used to work here."

"I'll see if I can get her for you. Want another Bud?"

"Sure."

He plunked a bottle in front of me and disappeared. A minute later he returned with his arm around a tall, broad-shouldered woman I would have instantly assumed had been a guy before the operation, or at least a transvestite. She wore snug orange pants that stopped halfway down her muscular calves, spiky heels, and a V-necked T-shirt under which rose a monumental bosom. She had pitch black butch-cut hair and a craggy pale face thick with mascara, pancake, and fire-engine red lipstick.

The bartender ducked behind his bar. Raybelle took the stool beside me. "You lookin' for me, honey?" she wheezed.

"I hope you can help me, miss."

"Miss," she repeated. "Heh-heh-heh. You're okay, honey. You wanna buy me a beer?"

"Sure." I turned to the bartender. He smiled and produced a Bud for Raybelle.

She lifted it and drained half of it. Then she pounded it down onto the bar and wiped her mouth on the back of her wrist. "Ahh," she sighed. "Only one thing better'n a good cold Bud." She dropped her hand onto the inside of my thigh. "So what's up?" she said. Then she laughed again, that evil heh-heh-heh.

I squirmed under her grip. "I'd like some information on a girl who used to work here."

"Lotsa girls used to work here, honey." She patted my leg and removed her hand. "Most of 'em don't stay long. What's her name?"

"Maggie. I don't know what her last name was."

"You got the hots for this broad?"

"No, that's not it. She married a friend of mine. She was killed recently. Murdered. I'd like to track down her parents."

Raybelle accepted this information without reaction. I might as well have told her that Maggie had invested in IBM stocks.

"What's it to you?"

"I'm the family lawyer," I said. "Some legal things to clear up."

She narrowed her black-rimmed eyes. "Like who killed her, huh?"

I shrugged. "That's police business, not mine."

She frowned. "Maggie," she mumbled. "Can't say I recall a broad named Maggie."

"Tall, black-haired, brown eyes. Quit about a year ago when she got married."

"Any scars, tattoos, or identifying marks?" She grinned. "Heh-heh-heh."

"I never saw her dance."

"You gotta help me more than that, honey. No chick danced here under the name of Maggie. Hell, I wouldn't let her. Maggie just don't hack it for a name. Whaddya think of Dusty Knight?"

"She was very good," I said.

"I mean the name, dummy."

"Good name for a stripper."

She nodded. "I gave her that name. Broad's real name is McGillicuddy. Imagine this: And now on the Night Owl stage, straight in from the Riviera in Las Vegas, ladies and gentlemen, a great dancer, a fantastic body, let's have a big hand for the beautiful, the sexy, the stacked—Gloria McGillicuddy." Her voice had become her announcing voice, lower, cruder, more suggestive. She cocked her head at me. "Heh-heh-heh."

"My ex-wife's name is Gloria," I said.

"Your wife probably ain't a stripper."

"No, she's not."

"I don't see how I'm gonna help you."

"My friend, who she married, his name is Marc Winter."

Raybelle gazed past me toward the stage. She shrugged. I sensed I was losing her attention.

"He noticed her when she pulled a hatpin on a couple clowns who were bothering her here one night."

Raybelle turned and frowned at me. "A hatpin?"

I nodded.

"Shit, I remember her. With the hatpin. Sure. Cool one, she was. Hell of a bod. Hang on, I'll think of it." She stared up at the ceiling and shut her eyes. Then she snapped her fingers. "Mona. That's who. Mona with the hatpin. Mona Mist. Mona was good. I was sorry she quit. She didn't tell me why. Married, huh? Well, that's what happens to 'em. They either get married or they get disgusted or they turn into junkies or drunks. You like Mona Mist?"

"The name, you mean?"

"Well, yeah. The name."

"Your name?"

"You betcha."

"A good one."

"So whaddya wanna know about Mona?"

"Her real name. Where she's from. Anything you can tell me."

She shrugged. "The girls come and go. Mona was good, though. Not much in the tit department. Great ass, legs that wouldn't quit. She could dance, all right. Real popular, Mona. Thing is, I don't get involved in the girls' personal lives. Live and let live, I say. And Mona, she didn't have that much to say. Kept to herself, pretty much. Came in, danced, left."

"Anybody here now who might remember her?"

Over her shoulder she said to the bartender, "Mike, you remember Mona?"

He shook his head. "I've only been here a few months, Raybelle."

She shrugged. "None of the girls been here a year. Big turnover in dancers."

"You must have records or something."

"Buy me another Bud. Lemme think."

I nodded to Mike the bartender. He obliged. I lit a cigarette and offered one to Raybelle. She waved it away. "Doctor made me quit. I got whatchamacallit— polyps—in my throat. Can't drink hard stuff, either. So I stick to the foamies and suck my thumb." She grinned lecherously. "Providin' I can't find somethin' better to suck on. Look. This is important, huh?"

"Yes. Very."

She swigged on her beer. "Okay. Hang tight, honey." She squeezed my knee for an instant, then waddled away.

Sally Flame by now had doffed her bra and G-string and had begun the dollar-bill trick, a minor variation of the theme of her predecessor. As I watched her, I was tempted to agree with Mike's assessment—you've seen one, you've seen 'em all.

Raybelle returned a moment later. She put an old-fashioned ledger book onto the bar and patted it. "I got it all here. Fellas I know tell me I gotta get me a computer. Like hell I do. What I need's in here. Okay. So I look up Mona Mist."

She opened the ledger, wet her thumb on her tongue, and began flipping pages. "Here we go. Mona Mist. Name she gave me was Maggie Burrows. That might not be her real one. I don't press the girls too close. They have to give me their Social Security numbers to keep me square with the IRS. That's all I care about."

She swung the ledger around so I could see it. Maggie had worked at the Night Owl from November to the end of June, a little over a year ago. Her salary began at $125 a week. By the time she quit she was making $350. "You gave her several raises," I said to Raybelle.

She shrugged. "She was good. I put her on more nights. Private enterprise, right? Don't forget, the broads make more than just salaries here."

"You mean the dollar bills on the railings."

"Heh-heh-heh," she cackled. "Yeah, that too."

"You mean—"

"They meet men. None of my business." She shrugged.

I took out my little notebook and copied the name Maggie Burrows and her Social Security number from Raybelle's ledger. "This should help me," I said.

Raybelle flopped it shut, tucked it under her arm, and turned to leave. Then she put her hand on my arm and her face close to mine. Surprisingly, she wore a delicate lavender scent that reminded me of a cheerleader I knew in high school. "Come back some time, Mr. Lawyer. Maybe we can do some business."

"I would've imagined you already had a lawyer, Raybelle."

"Oh," she leered, "I've got loads of lawyers. But a hard man is good to find."

She twirled off her barstool girlishly and strutted

away, giving her big bottom in her skintight orange pants a couple of exaggerated bumps.

It took me a moment to realize what she had said.

I finished my beer and watched the end of Sally Flame's performance. Then, oddly depressed, I left the Night Owl.

Charlie McDevitt and I were in the same class at Yale Law School. For a year we shared a ramshackle house on the water in New Haven, where we ate clams we dug ourselves and drank beer and entertained women. We sometimes even studied lawbooks. After graduation, I pursued my quixotic goal of becoming a truly independent lawyer in Boston. Charlie became a prosecutor with the United States Department of Justice, which he insisted was a logical stepping-stone toward his ultimate objective.

Charlie wanted to become a Supreme Court justice. In the nearly twenty years since we got out of law school, Charlie had not lowered his sights.

Several years ago he seized the opportunity to head up the Boston office for the Justice Department. "One step closer," he told me.

It was good to have him in town. We tried to coordinate our days off so we could fish and play golf together.

And we did each other favors, as friends do. In truth, he helped me far more often than I helped him. But he knew I was willing. And to keep our slates clear, we repaid favors with dinners at Boston restaurants. That way, neither of us ever felt indebted. It enabled us to ask for help more freely.

So when I called Charlie on Tuesday morning, I had no compunction about asking him to do something for me that I couldn't do for myself. "I need something out of your computer," I told him.

"You think all the data in the world are stored in government computers," he said.

"It seems to be."

"You think all I gotta do is poke a couple keys and I can tell you anything you want to know."

"You've always come through, Charlie."

"You think you can take me to Legal Seafoods for lunch and I'll do whatever you want."

"Maybe you'd prefer a trip to the North Shore. I've found some good spots up in Newburyport."

I heard him sigh. "Legal will be fine. What do you want?"

"If I give you a Social Security number, what can you give me?"

"Shoe size, whether or not they take cream and sugar, toothpaste brand."

"Seriously."

"Seriously, if I could access Defense and CIA and IRS computers, you'd be surprised. Scared, actually. It's kinda frightening."

"Can you?"

"What, access those computers? Naw. Not without a hassle. But we got pretty good stuff in our data bank. What do you want to know?"

I told Charlie about Maggie, her connection with my client Desmond Winter, and how I suspected that Lanie Horton was her biological daughter and that Nathan Greenberg's search for Maggie had somehow resulted in both of them getting murdered. "If I could just track down her family, I could take it from there," I concluded.

"I love the mahi mahi at Legal Seafoods," said Charlie.

"Good. A deal."

"So give me that number."

I read it to him.

He repeated it to me. "I'll get back to you."

I humored Julie for the rest of the morning, catching up on my paperwork and answering the accumulation of phone messages. I took her to lunch at Marie's, a little Italian place just outside Kenmore Square, where we split an enormous antipasto and a half-carafe of house wine. I offered her a raise. She accepted with a shrug, as if it was her due. She had a point. I still made more than she did, and she worked much harder.

Charlie had left a message on the machine while we were gone. "Got it," was the complete, unexpurgated text.

When Shirley, his round, grandmotherly secretary, put me through to him, Charlie said, "I ever introduce you to Artie Sheehan?"

"No. I don't recall the name."

"Good guy to know, Artie. Plumber who actually comes to the house and fixes things. As you know, water pipes and electric wires scare the shit out of me. We had a leak in the shower last week, so I called Artie. He came out on Saturday. He was telling me how he's trying to get over his divorce. He went to this restaurant in Wellesley one night, decided to have a drink at the bar before he ate. He says he couldn't believe how many great-lookin' women were in there. 'Charlie,' he says to me, 'it made me feel rejuvenated, just seeing them.' "

"Wait a minute," I said.

"What's the matter?"

"Is this gonna be one of your stories, Charlie?"

"This," he said, making the hurt drip from his voice, "is just something my plumber told me that I thought would interest you. If all you want out of this friendship is data from my computer, just say the word."

"Please accept my apology."

"Okay. Granted. So Artie gets up his courage and he takes an empty barstool next to a gorgeous blonde. 'Can I buy you a drink, miss?' he says. She turns and looks him up and down. Artie's not a bad-looking guy, actually, when he shaves and combs his hair. 'What do you do for a living?' says the girl. 'I'm a plumber,' says Artie. 'Get lost,' says the girl."

"Charlie—"

"So," he continued, ignoring me, "Artie's a little taken aback, but his ego's in decent shape. So he goes back to this place the next night and spots a brunette, also lovely. He sits beside her. 'Can I buy you a drink?' he says, because he figures that part of his line is okay. She takes a look at him. 'May I ask what you do for a living?' says the broad. 'Sure,' says Artie. 'I own my own business. I'm a plumber.' 'Buzz off,' says the woman. Artie gives all this some thought, so the next night when he returns to this joint, he finds a seat and gets the ear of the bartender. 'I been in two nights,' he says. 'Both times I try to start up a conversation with a couple ladies I get the brushoff. I use mouthwash, spray my armpits. I'm not really stupid, not totally ugly. What'm I doing wrong?' The bartender says, 'They ask you what you do for a living?' 'Yeah,' says Artie. 'What did you tell them?' 'I told 'em I was a plumber, mainly because that's what I am.' 'Aha,' says the bartender. 'That's your problem. See, the broads that come in here, well, stuff like that matters to them. You gotta tell 'em you're a doctor or lawyer or novelist or something. That'll impress 'em. After that, you're on your own.' "

I lit a cigarette and sighed into the telephone.

"Am I keeping you up?" said Charlie.

"I'm on tenterhooks," I said. "The suspense is killing me. Alfred Hitchcock could've taken lessons from you. What happened next? Huh? Huh?"

"Okay. That's better," said Charlie. "The next night Artie goes back. Spots a most attractive girl. A redhead, he told me. He sits next to her, offers to buy her a drink.

She asks what he does for a living. 'I'm an attorney,' he says. And, sure enough, she nods. 'I'd love a drink,' she says. So Artie buys her a couple drinks. Then she looks at her watch. 'It's getting a little late,' she says. 'Want a lift home?' says Artie. She says she'd love a ride. So Artie drives her to her apartment. 'Want to come up for a nightcap?' says the girl. Artie's about pissing his pants, he's feeling so lucky. So he goes up to the girl's apartment, and she, you know how it goes, she slips into something comfortable, and the next thing Artie knows he's in the sack with this gorgeous young redhead. Sometime later, they're lying there smoking cigarettes, Artie starts laughing. The girl says, 'What's so funny? Why're you laughing?' And Artie turns to her, and he says, 'You won't believe this. But I've only been a lawyer for three hours, and already I've managed to screw somebody.' "

"Another lawyer joke," I said.

"Ask Artie, you don't believe me."

"Okay, I believe you. What about that Social Security number, Charlie?"

"Got it right here. That's why I called you. The name that goes with that number is Margaret Gallatin Borowski."

"Birthplace?"

"White River Junction, Vermont."

"Parents?"

"Peter Charles and Josephine Katherine Borowski. Both currently residing in Bradford, Vermont."

"Siblings?"

"None."

"What about Maggie? What've you got on her?"

"She has never been arrested, that's really all I can tell you. You want more on her, it'll take some doing. I mean, I can try to pull some strings with Commerce or IRS, if it's worth it to you."

"What you gave me is a help," I said. "Appreciate it. Worth listening to your story for."

"Mahi mahi."

"Next week."

After I hung up with Charlie, I called Kat Winter's office. Her new administrative assistant answered with a snotty "May I help you?"

"It's Brady Coyne. Let me talk to Kat."

"I'll see if she has time for you."

Jesus Christ!

"Oh, Brady," said Kat in a moment. She sounded breathless.

"I get you out of the loo again?"

"No. I wasn't sure I'd hear from you again."

"I'm still your lawyer, Kat."

She laughed quickly. "Sure. Of course."

"Anyhow," I added, "the other night was interesting. Different. Intriguing."

"Intriguing?"

"Yes. Fascinating."

She snorted. "What kind of line is this, anyway?"

"No line," I said. "Look, Kat. Forget it, okay? The fishing was fun."

"Yeah. It was. You're not mad, then?"

"Nope. Course not."

"Well. Good."

"So want to come to Vermont with me?"

"When?"

"Tomorrow."

"Hang on a second."

I lit a cigarette. I smoked it. I stared out my office window at Copley Square, buried under a smog inversion. The sun burned dimly through, the color of urine. I smoked another cigarette. Julie came in, saw me with the phone to my ear, and arched her eyebrows. I lifted one finger. She nodded and left.

Kat came back on the line about fifteen minutes after I lit that first cigarette. "Oh, I'm really sorry, Brady. I had a call on the other line, and then I had to get a couple things cleared off my calendar. So I'm all set for tomorrow. What time will you pick me up?"

"Hey, great," I said. "Nine okay with you?"

"Nine is fine. What'll I wear?"

"Dress casual. I never go to Vermont without stopping to look at the trout streams."

"Sounds like fun," she said. "Is that why we're going? To explore trout streams?"

"I'll tell you all about it on the way up."

14

AFTER I HUNG UP with Kat, I put through a call to Horowitz at state police headquarters at 1010 Commonwealth Avenue. I figured his secretary might be under strict instructions to chill me, since the last time I had talked to the detective he had been decidedly hostile, but she took my name and asked what my business was.

"Tell Horowitz I have information for him on three North Shore murders," I said.

She did not seem especially impressed with the importance of all this, but after holding for several bars of "Moon River," I heard Horowitz's voice on the phone. He sounded as if he was eating corn on the cob.

"You're back on bubble gum, aren't you," I said.

"No willpower," he mumbled. "Whaddya got?"

"Maggie Winter in Newburyport, Nathan Greenberg in Danvers, Andrea Pavelich in Salisbury. Ring any bells?"

"Come off it, Coyne. Play parlor games with your adoring old clients. I know about the three killings, okay?

I even remember that you think Winter and Greenberg were connected."

"All three were connected, somehow," I said.

He paused. "How's Pavelich fit in?"

"She was Marc Winter's alibi."

"So you think—?"

"I don't know," I said. "They're holding the husband, I understand."

He paused again. I heard his gum pop. Finally he said, "Last I heard, they had a good suspect for the Winter case."

"Her husband. Marc Winter. He didn't do it. The Pavelich girl could've explained it. I told you he had an alibi. She was it. She explained it to me."

"Yeah, yeah. I remember you told me he was covered. The Pavelich girl, huh?" He paused. "Interesting that she got killed," he said.

"Makes it tough for Marc to explain himself." I lit a cigarette. "Anyway, there's another piece of this I thought you should know."

"Goodie," said Horowitz.

I told him about Nathan Greenberg's mission from Lanie Horton in Asheville, North Carolina, how he had tracked down Maggie Winter, who I deduced was Lanie's biological mother. "That's the connection," I concluded.

"So who killed who?"

"I don't know," I said. "I figure one killed the other, then a third party killed the first one."

"Like Marc Winter."

"Except he has an alibi."

"Had," said Horowitz. "He ain't got one now."

"I'm just trying to help," I said. "Do you know anything more about Andrea Pavelich's killing?"

He sighed. "The state police investigate all murders in the Commonwealth. We detectives are assigned our own cases, but we're expected to be familiar with all ongoing investigations. Okay? So we get copies of all the paperwork, which consists of big stacks of this extra-wide computer paper which doesn't fit into old-fashioned file cabinets, so it ends up all over the desk and jammed into drawers. So to answer your question, I haven't been assigned to any of these three cases that interest you, but, yeah, I know about them, more or less, and I got the paperwork here somewhere, and because I'm gonna switch you over to my colleague Moran in a couple minutes so you can repeat what you told me, I'll read you the paperwork on the Pavelich thing. Okay?"

"Okay."

"Okay. Hang on." I heard the shuffle of papers. I heard Horowitz mutter, "Shitfuck." Then he said. "I hate how this paper is all connected together and you gotta fold it right. Like a roadmap. I can never get roadmaps folded right. This goddam thing spilled all over my desk. Okay. What we got on Pavelich is this. Local cops got a call about eleven Saturday night from this Albert Pavelich in Salisbury. Says his wife is dead. They hustle out there and find this big guy on the back deck of their house. The guy's drooling, stumbling drunk, and the lady's quite dead. She was shot three times. Ballistics got two of the slugs out of her chest. A third one went through her throat, got a big artery, probably the one that killed her. A .22, which they haven't recovered. Automatic, they think. This Pavelich, the husband, they take him in. They aren't going to question him, the condition he's in, so they lock him up, get him sober, then they read him his Miranda. He refuses counsel and proceeds to deny doing it. Now the M.E. finds this dead gal has got old bruises on her neck, arms, and chest. Doesn't take too much checking around to discover that her old man, this Albert, used to beat on her pretty regular. Salisbury cops had answered more than a couple complaints over the years. Plus the husband has a little sheet. Mostly minor stuff. Driving under the influence, drunk and disorderly, battery on a police officer, stuff like that. Not your upstanding citizen. But not exactly a criminal, either. Just a big stupid asshole who drinks too much and has a bad temper. Statistically, your perfect wife killer. Likewise, they got it on good authority that the dead lady had boyfriends—"

"Marc Winter, for one," I said.

"Mm," said Horowitz. "Anyhow, finally Pavelich decided to get himself counsel, and the lawyer got him released, and he wasn't arrested, since they've got neither a witness nor a weapon."

"But they've got motive and opportunity."

"Yep. They figure he's the boy, and even though they've kinda botched the investigation so far, they're pretty confident."

"I talked with Andy Pavelich a couple weeks ago," I said. "Her husband saw us together and attacked me in the parking lot. I can vouch for the fact that he was a jealous and violent guy."

Horowitz was silent for a minute. "You don't suppose—?"

"He killed her because of me? Don't think I haven't thought of that."

"Hate to have that on my conscience."

"Thanks a lot."

"Look," said Horowitz. "This is enlightening and all, but none of these are my cases. I'm gonna get Moran on the line, who's handling the Maggie Winter case." And without waiting to exchange polite good-byes, he put me back on hold.

The telephone played "Bridge Over Troubled Water" while I waited, a schlocky rendition with lots of violins and no words, then segued directly into "Just Like a Woman," which used to be a good Bob Dylan tune before the Reader's Digest Orchestra got hold of it. Finally I heard a click, and a soft female voice said, "Mr. Coyne?"

"Yes. I'm still holding here."

"This is Detective Moran. What've you got for me?"

I repeated to her the connection between Maggie's murder and Nathan Greenberg and Andrea Pavelich. She listened to my recitation without interrupting. When I was done, she said, "That is really interesting. It doesn't help figure out who killed them, though, does it?"

"I suppose not."

"My best suspect on the Winter kill is still the husband."

"He's a better suspect now that his alibi is dead."

"His alibi might've been an accomplice."

"I talked to her. I don't think so."

"You think Maggie Winter was the mother, though, and Greenberg was tracking her down?"

"I'm planning on finding out," I said.

"Well, good for you. Let me know, okay?"

"Okay."

I hung up, more confused than ever, and impressed with the way police detectives avoided confusion. They simply zeroed in on a scenario and made it work for them, conveniently ignoring complications such as conflicting evidence. Jealous husbands tend to kill wayward wives. Ergo, Marc killed Maggie and Al killed Andrea. Hookers killed guys like Greenberg in motels.

These things were all generally true. They are the common things, and as medical and legal folks all agree, the commonest things most commonly do happen. A cliché, trite and obvious. But clichés achieve their stature by containing big chunks of mundane truth, as much as people like me hate to admit it.

* * *

I played "Shave and a Haircut, Two Bits" on Des's back door with my knuckle, and he called, "Come on in." I opened the door. Barney, the basset, waddled up to me, sniffed my cuffs, and finding no interesting dog urine smells, went back to curl under Des's legs.

He and Marc were sitting across from each other at the breakfast table. As near as I could tell, Des was reading the front of a giant-sized Cheerios box and Marc was reading the back.

"Grab some coffee, pull up a chair," said Des with what seemed to me forced joviality. "What're you doing in this neck of the woods at this hour?"

"I'm taking your daughter to Vermont with me. We may never return." I found a mug in the cabinet over the sink, filled it with coffee from the electric pot on the counter, and straddled a chair backwards. "I'm early, thought I'd stop in and see how you guys are doing."

"Andy's dead," said Marc.

"I heard."

"Al shot her."

"What I heard, they haven't proved that yet."

"Oh, shit, right. A lawyer. Innocent until proven guilty. Reasonable doubt. Burden of proof. Garrett keeps telling me that stuff, supposed to make me feel better."

I turned my head and looked hard at Marc. "You got something you want to say?" I said.

He returned my stare. "No," he said finally.

"Now, look," I said. "I wasn't the one who—" I stopped myself. Des was watching the two of us, his head swiveling rhythmically as if Marc and I were whacking a shuttlecock back and forth between us. I sipped my coffee. Then I lit a cigarette. "How're you making out, Des?" I said finally.

He shrugged. "I used to distribute solace to my parishioners like jellybeans. It's a little harder when it's close to home."

"I didn't do anything wrong," said Marc. "You shouldn't worry. Zerk's handling everything."

"Oh, it's not just you," said Des. "It's poor Maggie, too, and you, of course. And Kat. I worry about her, all alone. And, and . . ."

Connie, I thought. She was never far from his consciousness.

"Let's go fishing," I said to Des.

He nodded distractedly. "That'd be fun."

"I mean it. Let's make a date."

"Sure. We will. I'd like that."

I left it there. Des did not appear eager. I drained my mug, doused my cigarette butt under the faucet, and tossed it into the wastebasket. "Thanks for the java," I said.

Des did not get up. He waved vaguely at me. "Take care, Brady."

Marc followed me out the door to my car. "Look," he said.

"Forget it."

"I was out of line. It was me who—"

"It was Al, okay? It wasn't you and it wasn't me." I recalled the lecture Zerk had given me when I willingly assumed guilt for Andy's death. Now, as I repeated it to Marc, I understood it.

Marc shrugged. "I know you're right. It doesn't make me feel better."

"I don't feel great about it, either."

"I'm sorry."

"Forget it," I repeated.

He held out his hand. I shook it. Then I got into my car. Marc rested his hands on the roof and leaned toward the open window. "Zerk says even without Andy we're in good shape."

I switched on the ignition.

"It's not that easy," he said.

I shifted into reverse, then peered up at him.

"I lost Maggie, I lost Andy. What'd I do to deserve that? Huh?"

I reached through the window and gripped his forearm. "It doesn't work that way, pal. Ask your father for some theology on it. He'll tell you."

"He could use some theology himself." Marc straightened up. "Say hi to my sister for me."

I nodded and backed out of the driveway.

Kat was wearing a pair of tight jeans, faded almost white, and an orange polo shirt minus the alligator over the breast pocket. She wore sneakers with no socks. "Should I be more dressed up?" she said after greeting me at her door and inviting me in.

"You look terrific."

"But you—"

I was wearing chino pants, a plaid cotton shirt, and a lightweight sport jacket, no tie. "I am not exactly spiffed up," I said. "I've got to talk to some people. I'm trying to avoid looking like too much of a bum."

"Not that easy for you," she said. She picked up a shoulder bag and a sweatshirt and said, "I'm ready."

We took 495 south through the outskirts of Haverhill and Lawrence, old Massachusetts mill cities gone badly to seed. In Methuen we picked up Route 93 north. A little over half an hour later, in Concord, New Hampshire, we turned onto 89, heading west through pretty foothills and meadowland to the Vermont line, where we exited onto 91 north, paralleling the Connecticut River. In Vermont the mountains seemed taller and greener, the air cleaner, the farms more prosperous, the landscape more photogenic, the rivers more trouty.

Along the way I told Kat about my trip to North Carolina and my interview with Lanie Horton, and how

I had visited the Night Owl and tracked down Maggie's parents in Bradford, Vermont.

"You're a regular Sherlock Holmes," said Kat.

"You're mocking me."

"Not really. What I don't get is why you're doing all this? I mean, Mr. Garrett is defending Marc, and you didn't even know this Greenberg or Andrea Pavelich."

"It gives me an excuse to play hooky from the office for a day and take a beautiful woman on a drive into the Vermont countryside."

"You're patronizing me."

"Not really, Kat. It's as close to the truth as I can make it."

"Well," she said, "I'm glad. It's good to get away. And to tell the truth, all these murders so close to home . . ."

"Upsetting."

She shivered. "Putting it mildly. I didn't know the other two. But Maggie. She was a pretty good kid. And this Andrea Pavelich. Young gal. Couple little kids at home."

"She was Marc's friend," I said.

"I know. Doesn't mean she deserved to die."

We pulled into the little community of Bradford, Vermont, around noon. It consisted of a main street with a typical assortment of enterprises housed in well-kept brick buildings: hardware, groceries, real estate, bank, books and stationery, professionals, barber, gifts. We picked one of the three restaurants for lunch, and after we ordered I went to the pay phone and checked the phone book. I found the number for Peter C. Borowski. His address was South Road.

Our waitress, a middle-aged woman with a thick waist and thin neck, insisted we try the homemade mince pie. When she brought it, along with coffee, I got directions for South Road, which turned out to be a class-two road off a side road off the main road three or four miles north of town. I asked her if she knew Peter Borowski.

"Sure," she said. "Him and his wife come in here sometimes. They got a farm up there on South Road. You'll recognize it. Barn's been recently painted. Nice red, as if they were making it ready for people to come take pictures of. The house is white and could use some paint itself. They raise a few cows, some chickens, couple goats. They're more or less retired, I guess. Farm's kinda rundown, tell you the truth. 'Cept for the barn. They don't have much to say. Stick to themselves. Not big tippers."

I left a full twenty percent for our waitress, lest I be tagged a poor tipper.

"Did you call them?" said Kat.

"Nope."

"Why not? What if they're not home?"

I shrugged. "I didn't feel like telling them their only child is dead over the telephone. I didn't want to ask them if they minded my paying them a visit, because they might've said they minded. And if they're not home we'll go look for a trout river."

"Seems dumb," mumbled Kat, "not calling."

A Vermont class-two road is unpaved. The difference between a class-two and a class-three road is that the latter is not plowed in the winter.

During mud season, which lasts several weeks during the spring thaw, roads of both classes tend to be impassable to all vehicles save tractors, a situation that Vermonters accept with more equanimity than out-of-staters trying to reach secret trout holes.

South Road, three or four miles out of town according to our waitress, turned out to be nearly ten. That's the difference between country and city scale. It was unmarked, of course. Several winding miles later we came upon a crimson barn behind a flaking white farmhouse. I pulled my BMW behind a vintage Ford pickup. Half a dozen Rhode Island Reds were pecking gravel in the driveway.

Kat and I got out and chunked the doors shut to announce our arrival. From somewhere inside or behind the barn came the muffled moo of a cow. Otherwise, we received no greeting.

We climbed the porch steps. I rapped on the screen door. The heavy front door behind it opened almost instantly, suggesting that our arrival had already been noticed, if not acknowledged.

The woman's face was crinkled and ridged like a contour map. She wore round wire-rimmed glasses low on her nose. Her lips were thin and pale and lifeless. Only a fine straight nose and lively brown eyes hinted at the beauty of earlier years, the beauty that Maggie had inherited from her.

She held the door half opened and peered at us through the screen. "We ain't sellin'," she said. "We changed our minds. We've told the real estate folks a million times, they insist on sendin' folks over anyways. I'm real sorry if you had to drive all the way from Hartford or New York or whatever, but we just changed our minds about it, and it ain't the money, because we got some good offers."

I gave her my best smile. "We're not interested in real estate, Mrs. Borowski. We came to talk to you and your husband."

She cocked her head for a moment, then shrugged. "What about?"

"Your daughter."

"We ain't got a daughter."

"Margaret Gallatin Borowski? Isn't she your daughter?"

She squinted at me, then looked at Kat, then back at me. "Who're you?"

"My name is Brady Coyne. I'm a lawyer from Boston. This is Katherine Winter. Maggie's sister-in-law. You are Mrs. Borowski, aren't you?"

"Yes."

"Your husband is Peter?"

She nodded.

"And you don't have a daughter named Margaret?"

She pulled the door all the way open. "You may as well come on in," she said.

Kat and I followed her into the front parlor. It smelled faintly of propane gas, with an undertone of applesauce. A faded braided rug, dark upholstered sofa, wingback chair in a floral print, four matching wooden chairs, and a large television set. Mrs. Borowski took one of the wooden chairs. Kat and I sat side by side on the sofa.

"Peter's gone to the lumber yard. It's where he hangs around most afternoons. If he was here, I wouldn't have let you in. He's the one who says we ain't got a daughter." She looked from me to Kat. "You know Margaret?"

Kat nodded. "She was married to my brother."

"Was? Didn't last, huh? Figures."

"Mrs. Borowski," I said, "Maggie died recently."

She stared at me over the rims of her glasses. The corner of her mouth twitched, as if she were stifling a smile. Then she looked away. She shook her head slowly from side to side. "Peter says she's been dead for near twenty years," she said, talking not to me or Kat but to the dark corner of the room. "Twenty years, I haven't been allowed to mention her. All her stuff. Gone to the landfill. No letters." She flapped her hands randomly in front of her. "Dead? It don't mean nothing to me."

"I'm sorry," I said.

She rotated her head slowly to look at me. "Are you?" she said. "Are you really?"

"I liked her."

"Oh, she was a devil." She pronounced it "divil." Her eyes crinkled, although her mouth didn't join the smile. "Always figured one day she'd drive up in one of them fancy red sports cars. Liked nice things, Margaret. Always did. Wanted to keep up with the children in town. Oh, I never gave up on her. Not really. Tried to, but I couldn't. I never could talk to Peter about it. Can't talk to Peter about much of anything, truth to tell. Never could. When Margaret run away, though, it was like somethin' in him run away, too. Like they both was dead, and me stuck here with this empty corpse of a man and this memory of my little girl. Even her pictures he took from me. Every blessed one of 'em. Oh, she was a pretty one, all right, and too growed up for her own good. But I never figured she'd run off. Fifteen years old. Just a baby, though God knows she didn't look like no baby."

Kat leaned forward and touched the old woman's knee. "Mrs. Borowski, why did Maggie leave?"

"Why?" She compressed her lips. "You tell me, miss. You must be about Margaret's age. When you was fifteen, would you've wanted to get up with the sun to gather eggs before the school bus come bouncin' over this old dirt road for you? Would you've wanted to wear clothes that smelled like manure? I told him. I said we can't confine the girl. She's got too much spunk and too much savvy." She shrugged. "It was in the fall. One afternoon she wasn't on the bus. Last I seen her, she was gettin' on the bus that mornin', books under her arm, straw stickin' out of her hair. She waved at me and smiled like she always did. And that was the last I ever seen of my girl."

"Didn't you try to find her?" said Kat.

She bowed her head and snatched the glasses from her nose. She rubbed her forehead with her hand. When she looked up, tears glistened in her eyes. "Course we did. Peter didn't want to at first. He likes to keep personal things personal. But after she was gone a couple days, a fella from the school called, askin' if Maggie was sick. I just started bawlin', told him no, she was gone. So then the police come out, askin' a lot of questions I couldn't answer." She shrugged. "They never come back, though. I called a few times, but they said they hadn't heard nothin'. I never gave up. But after a while . . ."

Kat reached to her and touched the old woman's hand.

"So why're you here?" Maggie's mother said to me.

"To tell you about your daughter," I said softly. "It took us a while to figure out how to reach you."

"How did it happen?"

I hesitated. She narrowed her eyes and thrust her chin at me. "She was murdered," I finally said.

"Who done it to her?"

"We don't know yet."

"They gonna catch him?"

I nodded. "Yes, I expect they will."

"I s'pose it don't matter that much, now."

"Mrs. Borowski," I said, "I have to ask you a difficult question. May I?"

She gave a short, ironic snort. "You come and tell me my girl's been murdered. You think there's something worse'n that?"

"Was Maggie pregnant when she left?"

She nodded once. "I figure."

"You think she was?"

She shrugged. "It's why farm girls run away, ain't it? It's what I figured. It's why Peter wanted to keep it to ourselves. I figured Margaret'd be back. Go have a baby, maybe get married, maybe not. Maybe she give it up for adoption. I figured, few months, year at most, she'd be back. After a while, I give her a couple years. I kept makin' up stories so's she'd be comin' back pretty soon.

Even now, near twenty years later, I still got ways of figurin' it so's Margaret'd be comin' back."

"But you don't know if she was pregnant or not?" I said.

"No."

"And you never heard from her?"

"Never did."

"Thank you," I said. I stood up. "I am very sorry about this news."

Josephine Borowski stood and walked Kat and me to the door. She held it open for us. "You killed off my dream, Mr. Coyne. Do you know what that means?"

"I'm terribly sorry," I repeated helplessly.

She stood at the door. Kat and I went out.

"I ain't going to tell Peter," she said, standing behind the screen door. "He's got it all worked out for himself so's he can live with it."

"Be well, Mrs. Borowski," said Kat gently.

"I should've offered you lemonade," said Josephine Borowski to us as we went down the porch steps.

15

WE RETRACED OUR ROUTE along the class-three and class-two roads to the paved numbered route that led back to Bradford. Kat sat beside me, huddled against the door, staring out the side window.

"You okay?" I said.

"Oh, yeah," she answered without conviction.

"That wasn't much fun."

"No."

It took me a few minutes to figure it out. Josephine Borowski's daughter had run away. Kat Winter's mother had run away. It had been stupid, I realized, to invite Kat along for this trip, selfish of me to put my desire for her company on the long drive above her feelings.

Instead of getting back onto the interstate south of Bradford, I angled onto a secondary road, heading more west than south. The verdant pastures and hills were sprinkled with grazing cows and well-kept farms. The meadows glittered with masses of black-eyed susans and Queen Anne's lace. Every eight or ten miles we passed through a village. Each had its post office, a neat little white-framed structure topped by an American flag, its general store, with gas pumps out front, and a Protestant church, with a few no-nonsense wood frame houses clustered nearby. Generally a trout stream ran under a bridge just outside of town.

We drove without talking. I played a Telemann tape softly and allowed my mind to drift on the good ancient rhythms.

In midafternoon we came upon a crossroads. I stopped at the self-serve pumps in front of a village store, got out, and filled the tank of my BMW. Then I leaned into the car. "Want to come in?" I said to Kat.

"No. Go ahead."

The store sold yard goods, live bait, plumbing supplies, and pornographic magazines as well as food. I picked up a wedge of aged Vermont cheddar, a bunch of green grapes, a yard-long loaf of French bread, and a cold six-pack of Coors.

When I put the bag into the back seat of the car, Kat arched her eyebrows but said nothing. Outside the village I turned left, heading south on a narrow two-lane road that followed a tumbling freestone stream. A couple miles later I found what I was looking for—a class-two road that angled right, over the stream.

I parked in a turnoff beside the stream. I got out, tossed my sport coat onto the back seat, and picked up the bag of goodies. "Grab that blanket," I said to Kat.

She reached behind her for the brown army blanket I had kept on the back seat of whatever car I was driving since high school days. Without saying anything, she followed me along the edge of the stream until we found what I was looking for—a high bank topped by a grove of pines that overlooked a deep pool in the stream. I put the bag of groceries on the ground and Kat and I shook out the blanket over the cushiony bed of pine needles.

She sat on one corner, hugging her knees, her cheek resting on her forearms. I cracked two Coors and handed one to her. She took it without comment, held it against her cheek for a moment, then took a sip.

"Come on, Kat. Snap out of it."

"I'll be okay."

I shrugged. I took my fishing knife from my pocket, wiped the blade on my pants, and hacked off a chunk of cheese. Then I broke off some bread. I handed bread and cheese to Kat. Then I took some for myself.

"The guy in the store cut this wedge off a big wheel," I said. "Said it was well aged. Nice and sharp, huh?"

She nodded. "It's good."

I abandoned my conversational efforts. I ate and drank and tuned into the familiar outdoor cacophony: the buzz of locusts from a nearby meadow, the shush of breezes in the pines overhead, the distant staccato caw of a worried crow, the tinkle of the stream bouncing over rocks, and the complex mingle of woods noises, and after a while I more or less forgot Kat was with me.

When I finished eating I stood up, brushed the crumbs off the front of my shirt, and walked the few feet to the steep edge where a rocky ledge sloped directly down to the stream. A little pine-needled shelf jutted out over a deep, green pool where the currents funneled against the ledge. I lay down on my belly, propped my chin in my hands, and peered down into the water.

The pool was dappled in filtered sunlight. I could see straight down through the martini-clear water. I could count the rocks and pebbles on the bottom. It took me a few minutes to find what I was looking for.

Allowing for refraction, I guessed he was fourteen or fifteen inches long. He lay still as a waterlogged stick behind a small boulder near the head of the pool, a gray ghosty shape. His body and tail waved rhythmically with the currents. As I watched, he seemed to float upward toward the surface. He drifted backward a few feet, his nose nearly touching the buff-colored mayfly that floated above. Then with a suddenness that belied his otherwise effortless motions, he raised his snout out of water and gave a quick powerful twist of his tail that left a tiny whirlpool where he had been. The mayfly had disappeared. My trout sank back into the water and casually finned to his post behind the boulder.

A moment later the trout repeated the performance, and again, and I learned his feeding rhythm, and I knew that if I waded across the river downstream of this pool, where shallow water bubbled over a rocky riffle, and crept up the far bank, crouched low to present no silhouette, and took up a position fifteen feet down and to the side of that trout, and if I cast carefully four or five feet upstream of his lie, with a little right-hand curve in the leader, and if I had managed to tie on the right fly, and if the leader tippet wasn't too coarse, and if I mended my line properly so that the artificial would float naturally down to him at the instant when he was ready to eat again—if I did all that, perhaps this fish would drift under my fly and lift up his snout and flick his tail and suck it in. And if I were alert, I would raise my rodtip firmly and I would drive the tiny hook into his jaw, and if I gentled him just right I might lead him to my net. Then I would cradle him in my hand and twist the hook from his jaw and lower him into the river. I'd hold him there with his nose pointed into the current until I was sure that his gills were pulsing. Then I'd take my hand away and he'd pause for a moment, suspended at my feet, until he realized he was free. He'd flick his tail and dart back to his position behind his boulder.

Soon he'd forget what had happened to him. Fifteen minutes later he'd begin feeding again. But then if I cast my fly to him, something primeval would flash in the tiny bit of matter that passed as his brain, and he would not follow it. Maybe tomorrow, but not again today.

"What is it?"

I jerked my head around. "Jesus, Kat. Please don't ever sneak up on me like that again."

She settled onto the ground beside me, her hip and thigh touching mine. I could feel the warmth of her along my leg. She leaned her head against my shoulder. "I'm sorry."

"It's okay. You just startled me, that's all."

"That's not what I meant. I've been a terrible grouch."

"I guess you're entitled."

"No reason to take it out on you."

"That's what lawyers are for."

"Oh, Christ . . . What're you looking at?"

"Down there. There's a nice trout. I've been watching him feed."

She hitched closer to me. "Where? I don't see any fish."

I pointed. "See that boulder?"

She put her face alongside my arm to peer down the length of it. "Yeah, I guess so."

"See behind it? There's a gray shape?"

"Mmm."

"Watch it."

An instant later the gray shape lifted, drifted, and swirled below us. "Hey!" yelled Kat. "Oh, wow! Why don't you go catch him?"

I turned to look at her. "I already did."

"Huh? When?"

"In my mind. Almost as good."

"I don't get it," she said. "Fishing, I mean. You don't even eat them. So why do it?"

"Fishing," I said, "is just the most fun a man can have standing up."

I rolled over onto my back and laced my fingers behind my neck so that I could stare up through the pine boughs to the sky.

"What're you looking at?"

"Cloud shapes."

"What do you see?"

"Nothing any good. Abstractions. Cumulus and cirrus. I'm thinking."

"Good thoughts?"

"No."

"I'm depressing you. I'm sorry."

"It's not you," I said.

She got up on her hands and knees. She scootched down low, propped up on her hands, her ass sticking up behind her. She crept toward me on hands and knees and pressed her nose against mine. She widened her eyes and said, "Shape up, Coyne."

I rubbed my nose back and forth against hers. "Eskimo kiss," I said.

"I like American kisses better," she said. She gave me one. It lasted a long time and became complicated, what with our bodies shifting and adjusting to the contours of each other and our hands poking and stroking and further refining the fit.

After a couple years of that, or so it seemed, her mouth drifted away from mine. She arched her neck and I accepted the invitation. I kissed her throat and she moaned the way babies do when they are sleeping.

I found the little hollow at the junction of her throat and chest. I flicked it with my tongue. "Salty," I said.

"Good honest sweat," she murmured. "Wanna move to the blanket?"

I eased away from her and sat up. "No, I don't think so," I said.

She smiled and reached up to brush some pine needles off my pants. "Here?"

"No. Not here, either."

She rolled into a cross-legged position. "I don't get it."

"It's me," I said. I lit a cigarette.

"You wanted me. I could tell."

"Sure did. Still do."

"Then . . . ?"

"Forget it, Kat."

"Jesus, Brady. Are you some kind of prude or something? I never figured you for a prude. Some kind of hangup because you're my lawyer? Christ, this is the twentieth century, you know."

I shrugged. "Maybe I'm a prude."

"But that's not really it, is it?"

"Look," I said. "You want honesty? Okay. The truth is, I don't feel like participating in your experiment, that's all."

"What're you talking about?"

"Answer me a couple questions."

"Sure."

"When was the last time you had sex with a man?"

She opened her mouth, hesitated, then closed it. She shook her head. "A long, long time ago," she whispered.

"Your marriage. What went wrong with it? I met your Chuck. A nice guy."

"It just didn't work."

"What about the sex part, Kat?"

She nodded. "That's what didn't work. I couldn't . . . He . . . See, I get to a point and . . ."

I hitched myself closer to her and put my arm around her shoulders. She twitched and went rigid. "Kat, listen. It's no fancy moralistic code of honor. Nothing like that. I'm as dishonorable as the next guy. I can outwit my superego more often than not. And you are a most desirable woman. Okay? So supposing we moved to the blanket and proceeded as we had begun. Remember the night at your condo?"

She nodded. "Of course I remember. I told you—"

"If that happened again—"

"But maybe it wouldn't. This time I felt . . ." She closed her eyes. "I was almost there."

"Supposing it worked, or whatever verb we might choose. That would be special for you, wouldn't it?"

She smiled shyly. "Oh, yes."

"Well, see, I couldn't share that with you. I don't want to be your hero. I don't want you to fall in love with me because we succeeded in—"

"You are a bastard," she said.

I nodded. "That's what I've been trying to tell you. When we make love—if we should ever do that—it would be because we both had the same understanding about it. Maybe because it's fun. Maybe because we love each other. We'd have to agree. But not because it's a grim undertaking. I'd never agree to that. I'm not into grim undertakings. Not when it comes to sex. There's enough grimness in the rest of our lives. I'm not your man for that, Kat. Sorry."

"But you don't . . ." She stopped and hugged herself. Then she nodded. "I appreciate your honesty," she said stiffly. She stood up and went back to the blanket. I followed her.

We stuffed what was left of the cheese, bread, grapes, and beer back into the paper bag. We picked up the corners of the blanket and shook it and carried the stuff back to the car.

I followed secondary roads all the way south to the Massachusetts border. Kat said nothing, nor did I. I found Route 2, still called the Mohawk Trail at its westernmost end, and pointed my BMW east.

Somewhere around Orange, Kat said in a small voice, "I suppose you're right."

In Fitchburg she said, "I am kinda screwed up."

Near Fort Devens in Ayer she added, "But you're no prize yourself."

"I never claimed to be."

When we turned onto 495 heading north to New-buryport, she shifted in her seat so that she was facing forward, her back no longer turned toward me. "Did you find out what you wanted?" she said.

"About Maggie?"

"Yes."

I shrugged. "I think so."

"The girl you saw in North Carolina—she was Maggie's daughter?"

"That's my guess."

"So that lawyer—Greenberg—came looking for her."

I nodded.

"And he killed her?"

"Or she killed him. I don't know. That's the connection."

"I still don't get who—"

"Right. They couldn't have killed each other. That still puzzles me."

"And the woman, Andrea. How does she fit in?"

"The police seem to think her husband murdered her."

"Because she and Marc . . ."

"That's how it looks."

Passing through Georgetown on 133, a shortcut I knew, Kat said, "So it's all wrapped up then, huh?"

"As far as I'm concerned it is," I said.

As far as the police were concerned, of course, nothing was wrapped up. They had a decent circumstantial case against Al Pavelich. They had serious suspicions about Marc Winter in Maggie's death. They had, as far as I knew, not a damn thing on the knifing of Nathan Greenberg.

Three murders on the North Shore within a little more than a week of each other. Three victims with connections to each other. Three different local jurisdictions. Three different state police detectives investigating. Three different murder weapons, none recovered.

Maggie in the boat with a club. Greenberg in his bed with a knife. Andy Pavelich on the back deck with a gun.

It was beginning to sound like a game of Clue.

I called state police detective Moran the next morning and told her what I had learned from my visit with Maggie Winter's mother in Vermont. Moran claimed to find my information interesting and she thanked me in a definitive, final sort of way that conveyed her relief that my role in her case had terminated.

Which was okay by me.

I told Julie I was done with sleuthing and celebrated my liberation by buying her linguini with clam sauce at Marie's. In the afternoon I talked to clients and attorneys on the telephone, and when I thought I'd done enough of that to earn it, I called Doc Adams to set up a bass fishing trip.

I had a nice evening planned out for myself. I'd take about three fingers of Jack Daniel's in a big tumbler with plenty of ice out onto my balcony and watch the sea grow purple. Then I'd slide a frozen pizza into the microwave, timing it so that it would be ready at the same time as Jack Morris threw his first pitch to the Red Sox leadoff man on channel 38. Unless the Sox did some hitting I'd probably switch it off in the third or fourth inning, find something baroque on WCRB-FM, and fabricate some deerhair bass bugs for my trip with Doc. I'd flick on the TV news at eleven to see if Iran had finally succeeded in pissing off the entire Congress of the United States and to learn the magnitude of the Red Sox defeat in Detroit.

Then I'd shuck off my clothes, letting them fall wherever they wanted, and I'd take a long warm shower, from which I would tumble directly into my bed.

All of this was possible because I had no further interest in those North Shore murders. They were puzzles, all right. But they no longer puzzled me, because I had stopped thinking about them.

Somewhere between the Jack Daniel's and the pizza a guy named Ernie Cooper called me, and that nice quiet evening at home went right down the tubes.

16

I ALMOST DIDN'T ANSWER the phone. But I thought it might be Sylvie Szabo, returned early from her book promotion tour of the West Coast. Sylvie liked frozen pizza and the Red Sox, and she did exclaim wonderfully about the bass bugs and other flies that I liked to create.

Besides, after Kat, Sylvie's uncomplicated, fun-loving approach to lovemaking would have been welcome.

So I picked up the receiver and said, "Coyne's house."

There was a hesitation on the other end. Then a soft man's voice said, "Is this the lawyer?"

I sighed. "Yeah. Who're you?"

"Desmond Winter's lawyer?"

"Yes."

"I need to talk to you."

"Me?"

"Yes."

"You need a lawyer?"

"Well, yes. But specifically I need you."

"Who are you?"

"My name's Cooper. Ernie Cooper."

"Okay, Mr. Cooper. What's on your mind?"

"Not on the phone."

"Oh, Christ," I muttered. "Call me at my office, then. My secretary will make an appointment for you."

"No. I have to see you now. Tonight."

"Sorry. Can't make it."

"You don't understand."

"Well, hell, man, of course I don't understand. But I do know that it's after office hours and I'm sitting here in stocking feet looking at a half-full bottle of Jack Daniel's—"

"Look," he said. "Please. This thing has been eating at me ever since . . . Okay. Ever since Maggie was murdered. I've been carrying this thing around inside of me, feels like a shotput in my gut, and I finally decided I had to talk to somebody. And now I've got to do it. I can't hold it in any more."

"Did you kill Maggie? Is that it?"

"Oh, God, no."

"But you know who did, then."

"No. I don't know. I assumed Marc . . ."

"Then what?"

"That's what I want to talk about. Will you meet me?"

I took a deep breath and blew it out. "Ah, shit. Yeah. Sure. Where?"

He paused. "I live in Newburyport. I'd just as soon not be seen by anybody who knows me. There's a place near the beach on Plum Island—"

"No dice," I said quickly. "Someplace public."

"Why? Oh, I get it. You think—"

"I think nothing particular. Three murders and I get cautious. Meet me at the Grog. The upstairs bar."

"Everybody goes to the Grog. Someone'll see us."

"Unless you want to wait until tomorrow morning in my office, you'll have to take that chance."

"All right. The Grog, then. How long will it take you to get here?"

"An hour."

"I'll be there."

"What do you look like, Mr. Cooper?"

"You won't have any trouble recognizing me, Mr. Coyne."

"Why's that?"

"I'm bald as an egg."

He was sitting at the far corner of the four-sided upstairs bar at the Grog and he was right. Bald as an egg. He wore dark-rimmed glasses perched on a bulbous nose. He had a generous overbite and not much chin to speak of.

I took the stool beside him and ordered a bottle of Heineken from the girl in the Hawaiian shirt behind the bar. It looked like a wine spritzer that he was sipping.

"Thanks for coming," he said.

"You're welcome. Now tell me what this is all about."

He nodded emphatically. "I will. I want to. It's—I was with Maggie Winter that night."

"The night . . . ?"

"Yes. The night she got killed. God, I loved her. She was the most exciting woman I've ever known. I risked my family, my job, everything, to be with her. And now . . ."

"So when she threatened to tell your wife, you—"

"No!" His magnified eyes glittered fiercely behind the thick lenses. "No," he repeated more softly. "I told you. I didn't kill her. And I don't know who did. But I was with her, and I thought . . ."

"You're right. The police should know."

"The police? I thought if I told an attorney . . ."

"Any lawyer would advise you to tell the police. You have important information."

"But I don't know anything about her murder."

"You don't know that."

He peered at me for a moment. "Yes. I see that."

"Tell me about it, Mr. Cooper."

"Ernie," he said automatically. "From the beginning, you mean?"

"From the beginning."

"I met her one evening at Shaw's. That's a supermarket. It stays open late. My wife was sick. We needed a few things. I don't know my way around supermarkets very well. She made a list. She wanted salsa. You know, the stuff you dip Doritos in? Anyway, I went up and down those aisles and I couldn't find any salsa. I must've been talking to myself, because this dark-haired woman tapped my shoulder and said, 'Are you all right, sir?' And I said, 'What kind of store is this, they have no salsa?' So she pointed up an aisle and said that's where it should be, and she went her way and I went where she pointed. And there was no salsa there, so I said the hell with it, Jane could just do without.

"Anyway, I wheeled my stuff to the checkout, and the dark-haired woman was in the next line over, and she lifted her eyebrows at me and smiled and said, 'Find it?' And I shrugged and said no. So she finished buying her stuff and it was all piled in her cart and she started out of the store and then stopped and left her cart there and went to the aisle where the salsa was supposed to be. A minute later she came back and said, 'They're out. I'm sorry.' And I said, 'Well, it's not your fault. Thanks for looking.' And she said maybe the Market Basket next door has some, and I said it's really not important, so she shrugged and smiled and left.

"When I got out to my car, she was putting her stuff in the trunk of hers right next to me. So I went over to help her and we chatted a little. I told her my wife was sick and she seemed really concerned. A very warm person, I could see that right away. She said how it's really a drag when you want something like salsa and can't find it. That it makes you feel much angrier than you should. As if she could read my mind, because that's exactly how I was feeling. And maybe it was that anger, I don't know where it came from, because I'm not a very bold person, but I asked her if she'd like to have a cup of coffee with me. And she said she would and she smiled that great smile of hers, and I got this feeling, this tense excitement in my stomach. Do you know what I mean, Mr. Coyne?"

I nodded.

Ernie Cooper looked at me for a moment through those thick glasses. "I suppose every man knows that feeling," he said. "I had forgotten it until I met Maggie. So, anyway, we went to Friendly's—that's practically across the street. And we stayed there and drank coffee until the place closed, and by the time we left I was in love, Mr. Coyne. You knew Maggie, of course?"

"Not well."

"Well, believe me, she was a very lovable woman. Warm, caring, sincere. Not well treated by her husband, I might add. Anyhow, we walked out of Friendly's and Maggie opened her car door and this funny old basset hound kind of slithered out and went off into the darkness, sniffing around. So Maggie followed the dog and I followed Maggie, and we stumbled around in this field in back of Friendly's for a while. She was chattering away, so gay and carefree. And when we finally got back to where our cars were parked, we were the only ones left in the parking lot. She opened the door and Barney—that was her dog—he climbed back in and she—she reached up and kissed my cheek and thanked me for the coffee. That's all. She got in her car, started up the motor, and leaned out the window and said, 'Call me sometime when you find that salsa.' "

"So you did."

Cooper nodded. "I lay awake thinking about her, my wife snorting and snuffling and bitching in the bed beside me. The next morning from work I looked up Winter in the phone book and called and she answered and I asked her if she wanted some salsa. We met on the boat. We made love the very first time. And after that we met there many times. She shared my need for discretion."

"The boat doesn't strike me as a very discreet place to meet," I said.

He shrugged. "Maggie always said it was okay. I guess she and Marc had some kind of understanding. No one ever bothered us there."

"What about the night she was killed?"

"It was like all the other nights. She was there when I got there. We talked for a while and made love. She stayed there when I left. I never had that much time. Always worrying about getting home before Jane started to imagine things."

"What did you talk about?"

He waved one hand. "Nothing special that I recall."

"How did she seem that night?"

"What do you mean?"

"Was she distracted, moody, grouchy?"

He shook his head. "She was fine. Her usual self. Exactly herself. I've thought about that. I mean, she was about to die, but she had no premonition of it. She was no gayer, no tenser, no sadder. Nothing. Her old playful self."

"Did she mention any problem? Anything that was bothering her?"

"Just Marc. There was nothing unusual about that. We always shared what we called our spouse stories with each other. I talked about Jane, she talked about Marc.

Nothing mean, I don't mean that. We weren't complaining. It was just something we had in common, like all married people. You're married, aren't you?"

"No. I was once. I understand. What sort of spouse stories did Maggie tell you?"

He smiled, as if enjoying his memories of her. "Maggie thought Marc was seeing someone else. We laughed about that. I never had the impression that Marc's fooling around really bothered her. She used to say that they understood each other. Still, I think that if it hadn't been for the way Marc acted, Maggie would've been different. I mean, I think she would've been happy to stay faithful to him. That's how Maggie was. Totally accepting of how things were. She was just as happy either way."

"What time did you get to the boat?"

He gazed up at the ceiling. "Seven, seven thirty. I had dinner, helped Jane clean up the kitchen, and told her I had to go out for a while. Jane doesn't suspect a thing. She trusts me completely. I suppose she figures, a poor shnook like me, who'd be interested anyway, right? Anyway, it was probably around seven thirty. I left the boat a little after ten. Oh, I guess it must've been nearer ten thirty, quarter of eleven, because shortly after I got home the eleven o'clock news came on. I remember thinking that the best news was that Maggie and I had made love, and the worst news was that awful guilt I kept feeling."

"Did you ever drive by her house on High Street?"

He frowned at me. "Everybody in Newburyport drives down High Street."

"On that Sunday. The day she died. Did you stop in front of her house and talk with her that afternoon?"

"Oh, God, no. I wouldn't have risked doing something like that."

"Not even to set up a date with her?"

"No. We used signals. If the coast was clear for me to

talk, either from the office or at home, I'd dial her number and let it ring once. If she could talk, she'd call me
right back. Or else she'd do the same with me."

I drained what was left of the beer in my glass, nodded to the barmaid for another, lit a cigarette, and
looked at Ernie Cooper. He had barely touched his wine
spritzer. A quiet, cautious man. An accountant type.
Trustworthy, loyal, a good father and tolerant husband.
No match for a girl like Maggie. "And when you found
out she had been killed?"

He blinked at me. "I'm ashamed to say that my first
thought was that I hoped nobody would learn she had
been with me. Obviously, I'd be a suspect, but that
wasn't it. I knew I didn't kill her. It was that I'd be found
out and my life, quite simply, would be ruined. And
then, in a strange way, I was glad she was dead. She could
never tell." He passed his hand over his smooth dome.
"After that, though, I felt the sadness. It's very hard, Mr.
Coyne, to grieve privately, to have nobody to share it
with, no shoulder to cry on. So since that day I've grieved
over Maggie's death and worried that someone would
find out about us, and instead of the feelings diminishing,
they've become stronger. Until I couldn't bear it."

"A priest, perhaps? A psychiatrist?"

He shrugged. "I don't know any."

"You don't know me, either."

"You're the Winters' attorney, I know that. I know
Des a little. He's mentioned you. I know you're—involved in this case."

"Not really."

He waved his hand. "Anyway, I figured I needed
legal advice. Mainly, I had to tell someone. My own lawyer is a friend. Of me and my wife. I didn't want him to
know."

"And now we're going to tell the police," I said.

He nodded. "I know. I guess I'm ready. Do you think there's any way that this can be kept confidential?"

"That won't be a priority for the cops."

"I suppose not."

He followed me to the police station in his own car. Fourier, the Newburyport cop, was on duty when Ernie Cooper and I arrived there ten minutes later. I told him my name and he said he remembered me. He did not seem especially overjoyed to see me. I introduced Ernie Cooper, and Fourier frowned at him as if he looked familiar. We went to Fourier's desk. Cooper repeated his story, leaving out some of the details of how he and Maggie had met, but filling in extra details on the night of her death. He told the story the same way to Fourier as he had to me. Fourier asked a few questions I hadn't thought of—how Maggie had been dressed when Cooper left her ("Naked, sir. She was still in the berth"), if they had been drinking ("Not on the boat. We never drank before making love. Or afterwards"), drugs ("Of course not"), witnesses ("No. We always tried to be very discreet"). Fourier queried him closely on the time and his whereabouts immediately before and after his session with Maggie, everything Maggie said that night, anything Maggie ever said that might give a clue as to who would want to kill her.

Cooper seemed painfully eager to please. He stumbled around a little, got confused, couldn't remember, contradicted himself—in other words, he did all the things a distraught, innocent man would do, and all the things that a guilty man, having taken a couple weeks to prepare his alibi, would avoid doing.

I believed Ernie Cooper. Guilt was squashing him. But not the guilt of a murderer.

And I sensed that Fourier believed him, too. He told him that he would pass along his information to state police detective Moran, who was heading up the investigation. He told him that Moran would undoubtedly want to talk to him, but that he would ask her to use Cooper's office rather than home phone, and that, while he could make no promises, he saw no reason at that point for anyone needing to know what Ernie Cooper had been doing the night Maggie Winter was killed.

Tears came to Cooper's eyes.

Fourier nodded to me by way of dismissal, and said, grudgingly, I thought, "Thanks, Mr. Coyne."

I smiled. "You're welcome."

In the parking lot across from the station, Cooper pumped my hand. "I can't tell you how grateful I am to you," he said. "I feel so much better. I can live with whatever comes next. I'm going to go home now and tell Jane everything. I've got to trust she'll forgive me."

"Good luck, Ernie."

He drove off. I sat in my car with my feet stretching out the open door and smoked a cigarette. I wanted to ponder insignificant matters such as love and death, and how they so often seem to walk hand in hand. The butt burned down to my knuckle before I flicked it away and went to the pay phone I'd seen at the corner.

Kat answered on the second ring. "It's me," I said.

"Brady?"

"Yes."

"How nice."

"I'm just around the corner."

"Coffee? Drink?"

"Coffee. Be there in five minutes."

Then I went back to my car and sat and smoked another cigarette.

17

"WHAT A SURPRISE," said Kat when she opened the door. She was wearing faded blue jeans and a man's white shirt with the tails hanging loose. "What brings you to town?"

"Who, you mean."

"Okay, who, then."

"A guy named Ernie Cooper."

I followed her into the living room. "You really want coffee," she said, "or was that a figure of speech?"

"Really coffee."

I sat on the sofa and she moved across the room to the kitchen area. "Who's Ernie Cooper?" she said. Her back was to me as she loaded up her coffee maker.

"Maggie's boyfriend. He was with her that night."

Without turning around, she said, "The night she was killed, you mean?"

"Yes."

"Did he kill her?"

"No."

She came back and sat beside me. "It'll be ready in a minute. I was going to get it started when you called.

Then I thought maybe it wasn't coffee you really wanted."

"No, that's what I wanted."

"So what is it?" she said. "Something's bothering you. What's the matter?"

"I'm trying to start over again. Thinking about these murders."

"Why don't you let the police worry about them?"

"I'd like to. I can't help it."

"So what is it you're thinking?"

I stood up and went to the big windows that looked out over the moored sailboats in the Merrimack. Lights showed from some of them. Their reflections belly-danced on the rippling currents. "We've got three murders," I said. "I'm thinking that it's three times more likely that there's one murderer around here than three of them. I mean, most people don't commit murder."

"But which one? Do you think Marc . . . ?"

"No. Marc didn't kill anybody."

"What makes you so sure?"

"I'm not sure about anything. I just don't think he did. I talked to Andrea Pavelich. Anyway, he couldn't have killed her. They know where he was when she was shot."

"Her husband?"

"Big Al? A mean son of a bitch. Maybe. Except I can't think of a single reason why he'd want to kill Maggie or Greenberg. And of course, neither one of them could've killed Andy."

"They were dead before her."

"Yes."

She came and stood beside me. She leaned her cheek against my shoulder. "I like to look at the boats at night," she said softly. "It's so peaceful."

"I've made a lot of assumptions," I continued. "They

all more or less seemed to work. Then along comes Ernie Cooper."

"How does that change anything?"

I shrugged. "I don't know exactly. It just seems to skew everything a little. It knocked over my assumption that Greenberg made love with Maggie, for example. It's like a row of dominoes. Maybe Greenberg didn't even see Maggie that night. Maybe it wasn't even Maggie he was looking for. Maybe . . ."

She squeezed my arm. "Maybe you'd like your coffee now."

She moved away from me. I went back and sat on the sofa. In a minute she brought me a mug of coffee. I lit a cigarette and sipped from the mug. "Snooker told me he saw Maggie with a bald man."

"Snooker Lynch?"

I nodded. "Ernie Cooper is bald. So was Greenberg."

"So?"

I shrugged.

"You think too much," she said.

"It's a curse."

Kat lay her head back against the top of the sofa and looked up at the ceiling. "I'm sorry I'm so screwed up," she whispered.

"Me too."

"You're nice to still be my friend."

"Or at least your lawyer."

She sat up and turned to look at me. She was frowning. "No, I mean it. Most men . . ."

"Are just after what they can get," I finished for her.

She nodded. "It's true, actually."

"Maybe for teenagers, Kat."

She smiled. "You think everyone is like you."

"No I don't. Some people commit murder."

"Anyway, it's nice to have someone who understands."

"You think I understand you?"

She arched her eyebrows and smiled. "Better than most."

"It's not that I necessarily understand," I said. "Maybe it's just that I'm willing to accept. That doesn't make me nice. Or smart, either, for that matter."

"I think it's nice." She put her hand on the back of my neck. "I wish . . ."

I leaned forward to stub out my cigarette in the ashtray on the coffee table. Her hand fell away. When I sat back, she had retreated to the corner of the sofa, where she huddled with her legs tucked up under her.

"Tell me more about what you think," she said after a minute.

"About what?"

"All the murders."

I shook my head. "It's like some sweater that was all knitted, and maybe the sleeves weren't quite the right length, and maybe there was a stitch dropped here and there and the design was a little messed up, but it was okay. It kept you warm. It worked. And then you look at it a certain way and you know it just isn't right. I mean, I don't knit, but it seems to me that once you see something you spent a lot of time on, that you worked hard to create according to a picture in your head, once you see that it doesn't look right, you've got to tear it apart and start all over again. So that's how I feel about all of this. I feel like I'm sitting here with big snarls of yarn all around me and I've got to start putting it together in some new way that makes sense, so it'll look neater than the sweater I just ripped apart. I've got to get the old sweater out of my mind. I've got to find a new pattern and start over again."

"A pattern," she said.

"Yes. Reasons. Logic. Sequence. Cause and effect. I've got to see how everything fits together."

"If it does."

"Well, yes. But it has to."

"Things aren't always neat," said Kat. "There's a lot of randomness in this world."

"Well, I don't believe in randomness. I believe randomness is just a rationalization. Something for the simpleminded. A way of accounting for what we don't understand without needing to explain it."

"What about faith? What's left over after we understand all we can, the randomness, the unexplained, if we attribute it to God, or the gods, we can account for everything."

"I don't think we need God for that. God is just as bad an explanation as randomness. God is for lazy people."

"Or frightened ones."

I finished my coffee and put the mug on the table. I stood up.

Kat watched me out of big, solemn eyes. "Are you leaving already?"

"Yes."

She got up and walked with me to the door. "Going home to do some knitting, huh?"

I smiled. "It's a weakness of mine. Trying to make order."

She put her hands on the fronts of my shoulders with her head bowed. "Well, good luck, I guess," she mumbled.

I kissed the top of her head. "Thanks."

"I suppose you'll lay awake all night."

"It happens to me sometimes."

She lifted her face. "You probably don't want to kiss me."

I touched her cheek. "Thanks for the coffee," I said.

As I walked down the corridor from her door, she said, "Be careful, Brady."

I turned. She lifted her hand to me and then closed the door.

It was a little after eleven when I got back to my apartment. My bottle of Jack Daniel's was on the counter where I had left it when Ernie Cooper called me. I found the tumbler on the table by the sliding doors that opened onto my balcony. There was about a half inch of piss-colored dregs left in the bottom. I rinsed it out, poured in some more Black Jack, dropped in four ice cubes, and took it out to the balcony. I sat on the aluminum chair, tilted back, and propped my feet up on the rail.

I realized I hadn't eaten any supper. Somewhere along the way hunger had come and gone. The hell with it. I could think better on an empty stomach anyway, with maybe a little sippin' whiskey to lubricate the gears.

The big sky over the harbor was full of stars. The moon was low and big, a few days shy of full, and it lit up the flat black skin over the ocean and the islands scattered out toward the horizon. First booze, then coffee, then booze again. I figured they all neutralized each other.

I drank and smoked and thought. The breeze came at me from the sea, moist and organic. The bell buoy out there clanged its mournful rhythm. From behind me came the muffled city noises—the wheeze of traffic through the nighttime streets, the occasional punctuation of siren and horn, the almost subsonic hum and murmur of dense human life.

I remembered the Vermont woods, and my picnic with Kat, and how the birds and bugs and animals and river sounded, and how the pine forest smelled, and how my rainbow trout never missed his mayfly.

And while one part of my mind registered all of these surface things and wandered freely on its own associations, a different part of it looked for pattern and purpose in three North Shore murders, and a third part watched what was going on and tried not to judge it or guide it.

I might even have dozed, because the buzz of the telephone startled me.

I went inside and picked up the receiver in the kitchen. I tucked it against my neck and said, "Coyne," as I poured more whiskey into my glass.

I heard silence. "Yes? Hello?" I said again, taking the phone on its extra-long cord to a chair by the table, from which I could continue to watch the harbor.

After another long moment, a soft voice said, "Brady?"

"Kat? Is that you?"

I could hear her breathing. "Yes."

"What's up?"

"Oh, Brady . . ."

"Kat. Are you all right?"

She yawned softly. "Oh, yes. I'm fine. Sleepy."

"Feeling lonely?"

A quiet chuckle seemed to get stuck in her throat. "You got it all figured out yet?"

"I don't—"

"All the murders."

"I've done some thinking." I sipped my drink and looked out at the night.

"I didn't mean to," she said after another long pause. "She hit her head and her eyes . . . She was lying there, her head was all twisted, and she was looking at me and I knew she couldn't see me. She just slipped when I pushed her. I didn't mean for it to happen that way. But I couldn't let her tell. She was going to tell him."

I sat erect in my chair. "Kat?"

"Shh," she said. "You've got to understand. He couldn't know. She was going to tell him. She said when we got home she was going to tell him. I was just trying to make her not tell. It was just for him. Everything was for him. Oh, I miss her so."

"How did it happen?" I asked quietly.

I could hear her breathing. She didn't speak.

"Kat? Tell me how it happened."

"He came into my room. Oh, I loved him so much, then, and he touched me here . . . and he touched me here . . . oh, it feels . . . he made me feel so good when he came into my room at night when they were sleeping and I was sleeping and he'd wake me up touching me here and whispering and we had to be so quiet . . . And then she took me away and I was sick and it hurt and hurt and she was going to tell him, she said she had to tell him, and I said you can't. You can't tell him. It's not fair. I told you. It's a secret. And she said she had to anyway. So I pushed her, and she . . . her eyes . . . So I took her purse by the trains, I left her there and I got on the train and I saw the people running and rushing and yelling and I watched from the window and then the train moved faster and faster."

I fumbled for a cigarette. When I held a match to it, I saw that my hands were trembling.

"Oh, Brady. Oh I want you. But I can't. And you won't. Since he came into my room at night and touched me oh I just can't." She sighed deeply. I waited. "I tried to be so good," she whispered in a slurry voice. "For him. Perfect. I could make it all right if I was perfect. But then that man . . . He knew and he told her so I had to . . ."

"Greenberg?" I said.

"Oh, shh," she said. "Please. Shh."

"Did you kill Greenberg, Kat?"

"He wanted to . . . you know, he wanted . . . what they all want. All except Brady. Brady's always knitting, knitting . . ."

A cloud drifted across the moon. I heard Kat yawn.

"Blood, blood, blood. And she laughed at me, lying

there all sleepy-eyed, full of her sex, I couldn't let her laugh like that."

"Kat, listen to me. I'll be right there, okay? Don't do anything, don't go anywhere. Just wait for me."

"Her eyes, just like when the train, and her eyes, too, and it made me remember and I didn't want, I never want to remember, I sometimes forgot for a minute and it was like dreams underwater all fuzzy and faraway, and then she laughed so I had to make her stop before she found out. Brady? Brady? Are you there, Brady?"

"I'm here, Kat. And I'm going to come to be with you."

"No. You keep knitting." She yawned. "It's all soft and cottony here. See, oh, it was his fault, when he came to me and touched me here like this. So he had to pay the way I had to pay but he never knew so he couldn't feel it the way I always felt it. He didn't have it, that hurt in my belly, Brady, always there, and the buzzing always in my head. And that's why . . . I didn't think about her children, little things in their pajamas, but that wasn't fair, either, not when I had to . . . I was just a little girl, then, and I always felt like a little girl, and her children were crying at the blood but it was only fair that he should pay, too."

"Who, Kat? Say the names for me."

I could hear her breathing, quick and shallow, as if she had been running. "You should have made love to me," she said, her voice sudden and loud. "Everything would have been different. You should've fucked me, Brady. When that fish ate the bug you should've fucked me instead of knitting. Then it would've been all right." She sighed. "I was waiting for that. A long time waiting." Her voice softened and blurred again. "But Brady's gotta knit. Always thinking, no place for God, no randomness, no redemption, no salvation. No good stuff. Don't you think God, Brady?"

"No, Kat. There's just us."

"I tried. But even he doesn't think God's there anymore. How could I if he doesn't?"

"He loves you, Kat."

"God? God's not there. You told me."

"Not God. Des. Your father. He loves you."

"That's because he doesn't know."

"He'll forgive you."

"God won't, he won't."

"I'm going to hang up now, Kat. You wait for me. I'll be right there. Have some of that coffee and wait for me. Okay?"

"Wait," she said. "Mmm." She yawned. "Wait for Brady. Knitting."

"Kat, listen."

I could only hear her breathing.

"Kat. I love you. Wait for me."

"Love me, do. Oh."

"I'm coming."

I got up from the table and depressed the telephone hook. I held it down until we were disconnected. Then I dialed 411.

"What city please?" came a female voice.

"Newburyport. Hurry up."

"Yes?"

"The police emergency number there. Get it for me."

"I'm sorry, sir. You'll have to dial it yourself."

"Dammit! Okay. What is it?"

"One moment please." There was a click. Then a computerized voice told me the number. I disconnected, then dialed it.

"Newburyport police. Sergeant Casey."

"Send an ambulance to—shit! I don't know the name of it. The new condos on the river by the bridge."

"Who is this?"

"Brady Coyne. Listen. Katherine Winter, okay? I'm her attorney. Second floor, in the rear. Okay?"

"What's the problem?"

"Christ, I don't know. Pills or drugs or something. I was just talking to her on the phone. She's fading. Hurry up."

"Where are you now, Mr. Coyne?"

"I'm home. What's the difference?"

"Give me your address and phone number, please."

I gave them to him.

"Thank you," he said.

"Please hurry."

18

TWIRLING ORANGE and blue and red lights ricocheted off the brick and glass of Kat's building and illuminated the solemn faces of the gathered crowd. I counted three cruisers angled near the doorway with their motors running and their doors hanging open. A monotonous female voice rasped and crackled over a police radio. The ambulance was backed up to the door.

I got out of my car and jogged toward the building. I pushed my way through the people gathered there. "Excuse me," I said. "Let me through, please."

A cop held his forearm across my chest. "You can't go in there, buddy," he said.

"I've got to see her. I just talked to her, and—"

"Sorry, pal."

"You don't understand. I'm her lawyer. I'm the one who called. Please."

"Relax," said the cop.

I gripped his arm. His glance fell to where my hand held him, a warning. I let go. "Look," I said, taking a deep breath. "My name is Brady Coyne. I'm Katherine Winter's lawyer. I called the police about an hour ago because I was worried about her. I just broke several of your laws getting here from Boston. Now let me see her."

The cop shook his head. "You shouldn't've bothered."

"Huh?"

"Speeding."

"Can I please at least talk to somebody?"

He stared at me for a moment. "You're her lawyer, you say?"

"Yes."

"Say your name again."

"Coyne. Brady Coyne."

The cop turned to another uniformed policeman. "Get Fourier. Tell him the guy who called it in is here."

I waited there with the cop, the people behind me pressing close. I saw Fourier emerge from the doorway. He paused on the steps to blink into the lights, spotted me, and came over. "Hello, Mr. Coyne," he said.

"The ambulance is still here," I said. "I figure that means she's okay."

He touched my elbow and steered me toward a cruiser. I slid in. He went around to the driver's side and got in beside me. He reached down and flicked off the radio. "The ambulance is still here," he said, "because it got here too late."

I took a deep breath. "Oh, Jesus."

"I'm sorry."

"What happened?"

"You don't want to know."

"Oh, yes. Yes, I do."

He peered at me for a moment, then nodded. "Okay. She shot herself. She held the muzzle under her chin. She probably died instantly. The M.E. just got here."

I fumbled for a cigarette. I couldn't make the matches work. Fourier took them from me and got one lit. I steered the tip of the cigarette into the flame. I couldn't seem to hold my hands still.

"Take it easy, Mr. Coyne. You did all you could. You did the right thing."

"You don't understand," I said.

"No. No, I suppose I don't. But I trust you'll help me understand."

"It's my fault, see? If I hadn't . . ."

"Relax. We'll talk about it in a little while."

"She shot herself?"

He nodded.

"What—what kind of gun did she use?"

"A twenty-two automatic. It was beside her."

"Sure. I knew that."

"Of course you did."

"Did she—was there a note or anything?"

"Yes. It belongs to the medical examiner."

"Can you—?"

"I read it, yes."

"Who was it for?"

"No one. There was no name on it."

"What—?"

"It said, 'Now I'm going to be with her.' It wasn't signed, so they're going to have to compare the handwriting."

"Connie."

"Who?"

"Her mother. Connie."

Fourier put his hand on my shoulder and frowned at me. "You just take it easy, now, Mr. Coyne."

He stayed there with me and we didn't talk any more. I watched the lights flash and revolve on the faces of the people. The noises all seemed to mix together so that it seemed as if I was seated in the middle of an orchestra and all of the instruments were playing different tunes in different keys. It was very loud and it hurt my head.

After a while two men wearing white brought out a stretcher. A blanket was strapped onto it. I knew Kat was underneath. She was a small, shrunken lump. They shoved her into the back of the ambulance and it drove away. It moved sedately. It didn't bother flashing its lights.

Then a uniformed policeman came to the cruiser where Fourier and I were sitting. He and I moved to the back seat. The cop drove us to the police station. I followed Fourier inside. He took me into a closed room. There were bars on the windows. We sat at an oblong conference table in straight wooden chairs. Fourier told a policeman to bring coffee.

A minute later the cop brought us Styrofoam cups filled with yesterday's mud. He left and a woman came in. Fourier made a gesture at standing up. "Come on in," he said to her.

She had honey-blond hair cut short. She wore big hoops in her ears and a white sweater and dark blue slacks. She was slim and young and pretty. She sat beside Fourier, across from me, and held her hand to me. "Greta Moran, Mr. Coyne. We've talked."

I reached over and gripped her hand.

"You're the state cop."

She smiled. "Yes."

I nodded. "I'm very upset."

"Of course."

"I will tell you all about it," I said. "But if you don't mind, I don't want to keep repeating it. It's complicated. But I've figured it out."

"Can we get a tape recorder?" Greta Moran said to Fourier.

He nodded. "Sure. Hang on."

He got up and went to the door. Then he came back

and sat down. A minute later a female uniformed cop brought in a cassette tape recorder. Fourier fiddled with it, then put it in the middle of the table.

Fourier leaned toward me on his forearms. "Okay, Mr. Coyne. We're all set. Take your time. Try not to leave anything out."

I took a deep breath. "Kat Winter was fourteen when it started. That was 1971. In May of that year she and her mother disappeared together. Connie—that was her mother, Desmond Winter's wife—left Des a note. It said that they would be back, he wasn't to worry. Connie and Kat went to Winston-Salem, North Carolina, so that Kat could have her baby. Kat used a false name. You see, both Connie and Kat were trying to protect Des. He was a Unitarian minister. A highly moral man, given to quick and inflexible judgments, and a man with an impeccable reputation. If the truth were known, Des could've handled it. But Connie was trying to spare him." I looked up at Fourier. "You know Des?"

He nodded. "Go on, Mr. Coyne."

"Kat had her baby, a healthy girl. After her recuperation she and Connie headed home. This was in November, six months after they had left. They took the train. At some point during those six months, Connie had made a decision. She decided that Des had to know. On the train ride she told Kat. They would have to tell her father that she had gone off to have a baby."

I paused to light a cigarette. Fourier and Moran were watching me.

"They got off somewhere to change trains. They went somewhere where they happened to be alone. They argued. Kat said she didn't want her father to know. Connie insisted. She probably didn't know why Kat was so vehement. Anyway, Kat shoved her mother. Connie slipped and fell. She hit her head, or perhaps broke her neck. She died instantly."

"Jesus," said Fourier. "Fourteen-year-old girls get knocked up all the time."

"It was an accident," I said. "But Kat—I don't know. She panicked, I suppose. She took her mother's purse and got on her train. I guess they were unable to identify Connie's body when they found it. Another Jane Doe. Anyhow, Kat went back to Des, and by the time she got there she had decided how she would play it. Connie had sent her home, that's all. Her mother would be in touch, she told Des. That was the message. And she stuck to it. It must've driven her crazy, that awful secret. She dealt with it by doing all she could for her father. She tried to live up to his standards. She achieved. She took care of him. And she—for her, sex wouldn't work. It got all mixed up with her guilt and what had brought it all on."

I sipped my coffee. It was cold. I made a face.

"More coffee?" said Fourier.

I shook my head. "So for all these years Kat has lived with it and Des has waited for Connie to come home, and it probably would've continued that way until he died. Except meanwhile down in North Carolina Kat's daughter had been adopted and was growing up and falling in love and getting married. She got pregnant. Her child was stillborn. Her doctor suspected genetic problems and tried to get a medical history of her and her husband. Lanie Horton—that's Kat's daughter's name—knowing she was adopted, hired a local lawyer to track down her parents. That was—"

"Greenberg," said Moran. "Nathan Greenberg, the guy who—"

"Right," I said. "He thought he had it figured out. So he came to Newburyport looking for Kat. I thought it was Maggie who was Lanie's mother. They looked alike. Tall, dark. But it was Kat. Anyway, Greenberg flew into Boston. It was on a weekend. He tried to call me, but I wasn't in. He took a motel room in Danvers and then drove to Newburyport. He went to Des's house and saw Maggie outside. I suppose he assumed Maggie was Kat. As I said, there was a resemblance between Maggie and Lanie Horton. Anyhow, he introduced himself and asked if she was Katherine Winter. Maggie said no, of course, but she told him how to reach Kat. I figure he called Kat and gave her an idea of what was on his mind. From what people have told me about Greenberg, he must've invited her to his motel. Maybe he had decided to blackmail her. Maybe he just hoped for a seduction. Maybe it was Kat's idea that they meet there. Maybe she intended to kill him all along. Anyway, she went there with a serrated kitchen knife in her purse. They talked. Greenberg told her that he had spoken with Maggie. So after Kat killed him, she had to find Maggie, because Maggie was the only one who could link Kat with Nate Greenberg."

"My God!" breathed Moran.

I stood up and began to move around the room. "So Kat went to the boat—"

"Please, Mr. Coyne," said Fourier, gesturing to the chair. "The recorder."

I nodded. "Sorry." I sat down again. "So Kat went to the boat. I suppose she knew that's where Maggie met her lover." I looked up at Fourier. "Ernie Cooper?"

He nodded. "Who you brought in earlier this evening."

"Yeah. Anyway, Kat waited until Cooper left and Maggie was alone on the boat. She picked up the priest—the club they kill fish with—and went below. Maggie was in the berth. Kat clubbed her to death. A little while later Marc came along with his lover, Andrea Pavelich. They went down and saw Maggie's body. Marc took Andy home, then drove back and called the police."

I stopped and slumped down in my chair.

"Coffee?" said Fourier.

I lifted my hand. "No. Give me a minute. This is hard."

He nodded.

"You understand," I said, "this is mostly surmise on my part. All the thinking I've done on it plus what Kat said to me on the phone before—before she shot herself. She had taken pills, I think. She wasn't entirely coherent. I think you'll find that the .22 automatic she shot herself with was the same weapon that killed Andy Pavelich."

"Why kill her?" said Moran.

"Kat blamed Marc. She loved him and she hated him. Some twisted part of her was able to persuade her that he was the one that had caused it all and he was the one who deserved to suffer for it. She saw him as they grew up. That he didn't seem to suffer the way she did. It was not her original intention, probably, that Marc be suspected of Maggie's death. But when Kat realized he was, she felt it was just. So when she learned—when I told her —that Andy Pavelich was Marc's alibi, Kat killed her, too."

Moran nodded. "Okay," she said. "I can see that. So why did she kill herself tonight?"

"Me," I said, spreading my hands. "She thought I was figuring it out. And I think she was in love with me."

"Oh, I don't think you should—"

I nodded quickly. "I'm not. Kat was sick. Who wouldn't be, carrying that load around for eighteen or nineteen years? Something was bound to break inside of her sometime. She was all twisted up. I just happened to come along. Still, I wish it had been somebody else."

Fourier was staring at me. "Is that it, Mr. Coyne?"

I shrugged. "Except for one thing."

"Go ahead."

"The thing that made her secret so awful, the thing that her father couldn't know, the thing that made her feel justified in killing Andrea Pavelich. Don't you see?"

Moran and Fourier stared at me. Then Moran's mouth opened. "Oh, God," she whispered.

"Yeah. Marc. I feel stupid that I didn't see it quicker. Lanie Horton, Kat's daughter, she's tall and dark, just like Maggie. That's what fooled me. But Kat is tall, too. And Marc is dark. Kat's brother was the one that came to her bed at night. It was his baby she was carrying."

Fourier and Moran asked me a lot of questions, which I answered as well as I could. Finally he looked at her and said, "Well, it's really just a lot of conjecture."

She nodded. "But it fits together better than anything else we've been able to come up with. And there are several things we can do to pin it down."

"Sure. Ballistics on that .22, for one thing. We done with him?"

She looked at me. "For now."

I waited around the Newburyport police station, drinking coffee and smoking, until Fourier brought me a typed copy of my statement. I read it through and signed it.

A policeman drove me back to Kat's building, where I had left my car. I sat in it for a while, staring at the doorway where I had seen Kat's body being lugged out. After a while the sky began to turn silver and the boats moored in the river changed from silhouettes to three-dimensional objects.

I started up my car and drove to Des's house. It was something I had to do.

Marc met me at the door. He held a can of beer in his hand. He gestured with a jerk of his head for me to come in. Barney the basset was sleeping beside the stove. He opened his eyes for a moment, rolled them at me, sighed, and closed them again.

"My father's asleep," said Marc. "Get you something?"

I shook my head. We sat across from each other at the kitchen table. Marc stared down at the beer can he was holding in both hands.

"The doctor was here. Gave him a sedative. He's very shook up."

"What does he know?"

He looked up at me. "Know?"

I nodded. "What did they tell him?"

He shrugged. "That Kat shot herself. They showed him the note and he identified her handwriting. Then they took him to the hospital to identify her body. Then they brought him back and the doctor came and gave him pills. He's upstairs."

"Did they say anything about your mother?"

Marc frowned. "What about her?"

I shook my head. "Nothing. Just wondering." I stared hard at him.

He returned my gaze, a puzzled look on his face. "What is it, Brady?"

"You don't know, do you?"

"Look, this has been a tough night. I'm in no mood for puzzles."

"Where Kat and your mother went?"

"God. That was a long time ago. What's that got to do with anything?"

"Everything," I said. "And one of us, you or I, has to decide how much to tell your father."

He narrowed his eyes. "Well, maybe you better tell me first."

"I'll keep it simple. You knocked up your sister. Her mother took her south to have her baby. When Connie threatened to tell your father, Kat killed her. When her baby—hers and yours—grew up, she sent a detective looking for her parents. The detective talked to your wife. So Kat killed both of them, Maggie and Greenberg, and then she killed your girlfriend, too, just for good measure."

Marc's eyes never left my face. He registered no expression. After a long minute, he whispered, "I didn't know."

I lit a cigarette and shrugged.

"You want me to tell my father all this?"

"He's your father."

"He's an old man."

"He's a man."

"What good would it do to tell him?"

"That," I said, "may not be the question."

"She hated me, didn't she?"

"Kat?"

He nodded.

"She probably did. And loved you, too."

"You don't think I suffered? Making—doing that with your own sister? Knowing what I did?"

"Kat suffered worse."

"What do you think of me, Brady?"

"It doesn't really matter what I think," I said.

EPILOGUE

I TOOK the coward's way out. I got Dr. Hendrick's phone number from Victoria Jones and called him. His secretary said he was with a patient. When I told her I was a lawyer calling from Boston, and that I had information he needed on Lanie Horton, she said she'd see if she could interrupt him.

A moment later a deep, gentle voice said, "Paul Hendrick."

"Doctor," I said, "my name is Brady Coyne. I'm calling about Lanie Horton."

"Yes?" I visualized him, somehow, wearing a waistcoat and bow tie, with piercing blue eyes behind rimless glasses low on his nose, a thin white mustache, white crewcut.

"You needed a medical history on her parents."

"Go on."

I cleared my throat. "Her parents—her mother and father—well, they're siblings."

"Oh, my."

"Well, I just wanted you to know."

"And you wanted me to tell her."

"I guess somebody should."

"Doctors are good at conveying bad news, is that it?"

"Lawyers have to do that sometimes, too."

"I'll take care of it, Mr. Coyne. Thank you, I guess."

Constance skimmed smoothly across the furrowed sea. After I finished filleting the three blues that we kept and stowing the tackle, I went forward and stood beside Des. He held the wheel in one confident hand, squinting through the rain-spattered windshield, straining to find the landmarks on the misted shore.

I handed him a beer. "Thank you," he said.

"It was a good day."

"Last one of the season, I expect. They're schooling up for their migration. We were lucky to find them. They'll be gone in a week."

"You haven't lost your nose for bluefish, Des."

He smiled and nodded. "They showed me her picture, you know."

I waited.

"The police. They were very kind. They got a photograph over their computer from New York. They had to know if it was her."

"Connie?"

He nodded. "They found her in a restroom in Grand Central Station. It was November the ninth, 1971. The day Katherine came home. They couldn't identify her. Nobody knew who she was. Nobody filed a missing person on her. Nobody went looking for her. After a while they buried her somewhere. She had a fractured skull. Jane Doe. My Connie. An anonymous corpse . . ."

I wondered what Marc had told him, what else he knew.

I put my arm around his shoulder. "I'm sorry, old friend."

He shook his head. "No, don't be. You don't negotiate with life. You take what you get. This has been mine. I can't complain. I have many things to be grateful for."

He stared at the sea. I couldn't think of anything to say.

"She didn't leave me, you see," he said after several minutes. "I always hoped to know about that before I died. She never stopped loving me. She was coming back to me."

He began the wide turn that would take us into the mouth of the Merrimack, to the slip in the Newburyport marina where *Constance* rode out storms and tides.

"The other thing I'm grateful for," said the old man, "is the nineteen years of hope I had. I was lucky to have that."

I sipped my beer and studied the sea. Desmond Winter considered himself a lucky man.

What did that make me?